I0763296

PRAISE FOR
CARLTON MELLICK III

"Easily the craziest, weirdest, strangest, funniest, most obscene writer in America."
—*GOTHIC MAGAZINE*

"Carlton Mellick III has the craziest book titles... and the kinkiest fans!"
—CHRISTOPHER MOORE, author of *The Stupidest Angel*

"If you haven't read Mellick you're not nearly perverse enough for the twenty first century."
—JACK KETCHUM, author of *The Girl Next Door*

"Carlton Mellick III is one of bizarro fiction's most talented practitioners, a virtuoso of the surreal, science fictional tale."
—CORY DOCTOROW, author of *Little Brother*

"Bizarre, twisted, and emotionally raw—Carlton Mellick's fiction is the literary equivalent of putting your brain in a blender."
—BRIAN KEENE, author of *The Rising*

"Carlton Mellick III exemplifies the intelligence and wit that lurks between its lurid covers. In a genre where crude titles are an art in themselves, Mellick is a true artist."
—*THE GUARDIAN*

"Just as Pop had Andy Warhol and Dada Tristan Tzara, the bizarro movement has its very own P. T. Barnum-type practitioner. He's the mutton-chopped author of such books as *Electric Jesus Corpse* and *The Menstruating Mall*, the illustrator, editor, and instructor of all things bizarro, and his name is Carlton Mellick III."
—*DETAILS MAGAZINE*

"The most original novelist working today? The most outrageous? The most unpredictable? These aren't easy superlatives to make; however, Carlton Mellick may well be all of those things, behind a canon of books that all irreverently depart from the form and concepts of traditional novels, and adventure the reader into a howling, dark fantasyland of the most bizarre, over-the-top, and mind-warping inventiveness."
—EDWARD LEE, author of *Header*

"Discussing Bizarro literature without mentioning Mellick is like discussing weird-ass muttonchopped authors without mentioning Mellick."
—*CRACKED.COM*

"Carlton is an acquired taste, but he hooks you like a drug."
—HUNTER SHEA, author of *Forest of Shadows*

"Mellick's career is impressive because, despite the fact that he puts out a few books a year, he has managed to bring something new to the table every time... Every Mellick novel is packed with more wildly original concepts than you could find in the current top ten *New York Times* bestsellers put together."
—*VERBICIDE*

"Mellick's guerrilla incursions combine total geekboy fandom and love with genuine, unbridled outsider madness. As such, it borders on genius, in the way only true outsider art can."
—*FANGORIA*

Also by
Carlton Mellick III

Satan Burger
Electric Jesus Corpse (Fan Club Exclusive)
Sunset With a Beard (stories)
Razor Wire Pubic Hair
Teeth and Tongue Landscape
The Steel Breakfast Era
The Baby Jesus Butt Plug
Fishy-fleshed
The Menstruating Mall
Ocean of Lard (with Kevin L. Donihe)
Punk Land
Sex and Death in Television Town
Sea of the Patchwork Cats
The Haunted Vagina
Cancer-cute (Fan Club Exclusive)
War Slut
Sausagey Santa
Ugly Heaven
Adolf in Wonderland
Ultra Fuckers
Cybernetrix
The Egg Man
Apeshit
The Faggiest Vampire
The Cannibals of Candyland
Warrior Wolf Women of the Wasteland
The Kobold Wizard's Dildo of Enlightenment +2
Zombies and Shit
Crab Town
The Morbidly Obese Ninja
Barbarian Beast Bitches of the Badlands
Fantastic Orgy (stories)
I Knocked Up Satan's Daughter
Armadillo Fists

The Handsome Squirm
Tumor Fruit
Kill Ball
Cuddly Holocaust
Hammer Wives (stories)
Village of the Mermaids
Quicksand House
Clusterfuck
Hungry Bug
Tick People
Sweet Story
As She Stabbed Me Gently in the Face
ClownFellas: Tales of the Bozo Family
Bio Melt
Every Time We Meet at the Dairy Queen,
Your Whole Fucking Face Explodes
The Terrible Thing That Happens
Exercise Bike
Spider Bunny
The Big Meat
Parasite Milk
Stacking Doll
Neverday
The Boy with the Chainsaw Heart
Mouse Trap
Snuggle Club
The Bad Box
Full Metal Octopus
Goblins on the Other Side
The Girl with the Barbed Wire Hair
You Always Try to Kill Me in Your Dreams
Glass Children
Why I Married a Clown Girl From the Dimension of Death
Apeship
Scorpion Ranch

KISS FUCK MARRY KILL

CARLTON MELLICK III

ERASERHEAD PRESS
PORTLAND, OREGON

ERASERHEAD PRESS
P.O. BOX 10065
PORTLAND, OR 97296

WWW.ERASERHEADPRESS.COM

ISBN: 978-1-62105-366-8

Cover concept by Anton Vilkin

Printed in the USA.

AUTHOR'S NOTE

I have always been fascinated by ethics, mostly when it comes to navigating complex moral dilemmas. I've found that my morals tend to be somewhat pragmatic compared to a lot of people's. I prefer to keep my morals simple. For example: I treat everyone with respect. No exceptions. There's not a single person, no matter what they've done or what they believe, that shouldn't be treated with respect. It sounds obvious enough, but I don't know many people who stick to this hard rule.

I'm a big fan of the trolley problem. I'm sure you know the one. It's the hypothetical thought experiment where a runaway trolley is about to kill five people but you have the option to pull a lever that would divert the trolley onto a track that would kill only one person. Would you pull the lever? There's a website called absurd trolley problems that has multiple versions of this thought experiment. From a trolley that is about to kill a baby but you can redirect it to kill five elderly people, to five people tied to a track but you can divert it to kill four people, to five people tied to a track but you can divert it to kill one family member. In every situation, my decision would always be the same: never pull the lever. In the original trolley problem, I don't see pulling the lever as saving five people. I only see it as murdering one person. As I said, I keep my morals simple. I would never pull the lever under any circumstance if it requires murdering someone else, no matter who it is or who I'd be saving.

The social game *Fuck Marry Kill*, or the PG version *Kiss Marry Kill*, is another hypothetical thought experiment. When I wrote this book, I wanted to see how people would handle this dilemma in real life. Only I didn't want it to be from the perspective of the victims. I wanted to focus on the person who has control of the lever. Because I think that would be the absolute worst position to be in.

While it might seem like it, this book isn't trying to make any kind of political statement. My books come across as political at times, but I don't have any agenda behind the books I write. I just like to put characters in situations that are shitty for everyone involved. Honestly, it's what I like most about writing stories.

So here it is, *Kiss Fuck Marry Kill*, my 70th book. I hope you enjoy it.

—Carlton Mellick III 11/11/25, 5:07pm

CHAPTER ONE

I hate being a man. Everything about being a man disgusts me. I hate the way men look, the way our bodies are shaped like thick, bulbous lumps of ugliness. I hate how our testicles stick to the sides of our thighs on hot, humid days. I hate getting erections in class for no reason whatsoever. I hate having facial hair, armpit hair, chest hair, and pretty much all the hair that grows out of my coarse, greasy skin in unsightly patches. If people wouldn't make fun of me for it, I would laser off every inch of hair from my entire body, even my pubic hair, to be as smooth and shiny as a bikini model. But I'm a coward. I would never do anything that would make me stand out.

If I were born a woman, then maybe I wouldn't find myself revolting. I wouldn't even need to be an attractive woman, as some guys have been known to fantasize about. I would just need to look the exact opposite of a man. But I'm not sure I want to be a woman, either. Women don't exactly have it easy, both biologically and socially. I wouldn't want to menstruate or give birth, be treated like a sex object, or have to work harder to succeed in the world. I wouldn't want to be called a slut or a bitch or a Karen or a fat chick or a cock sleeve or a cum dumpster. I wouldn't want to have to dread being devalued by society for gaining weight or getting old. And, worst of all, I wouldn't want to be expected to marry a man.

Part of me wishes that I had close female friends so that I could surround myself with femininity, but women don't want anything to do with me. Whenever I try to make friends with a woman, she will just think I'm hitting on her and am just after her for sex. Where I go to school, all the women on campus are suspicious of men. There have been too many cases of sexual harassment and sexual assault for them to rest easy while in the company of my gender.

And they are right to be cautious. Living in the male dorm, I am surrounded by misogynistic guys who only talk about women as a means of getting laid, as goals to pursue. They divide up women among them to claim their targets, trading them like baseball cards, to make sure they don't get cockblocked by their friends once they're ready to make their move. It disgusts me. It makes me ashamed to be who I am. And the part that I hate the most is the fact that I don't have the courage to stand up to them. I don't have the guts to tell them off or tell them that their behavior is all wrong. Because, deep down, I know I am exactly like them.

I wake up to the sound of a woman screaming. When I open my eyes, I see her standing over me, pounding on a door and begging to be let out. All I see are her panties above me. Her legs straddling my torso, spread wide enough to give me a clear view of her white sheer underwear fitting tightly to her crotch. Her long skirt encompasses me like a blanket.

"Can anyone hear me?" she cries. "Let me out!"

I have no idea where I am or how I got here. I'm lying on a hard linoleum floor next to what I assume is the entrance to the room we're in. She doesn't seem to notice me lying here, or doesn't seem to be concerned with me, because she probably thinks I'm still asleep. I don't know what to do in this situation. My mind floods with worry. But not so much about waking up in this unfamiliar place. I'm more concerned that I'm inside this woman's skirt and looking up at her underwear. I feel like such a creep just by having seen them, even though it wasn't my intention. I'm not sure if I should let her know that I'm awake or just keep pretending to be asleep until she moves. I close my eyes and turn my head, trying to seem as unconscious as possible. But I know this will only make me seem even more suspicious if she notices that I'm only pretending. I am not a creepy guy. I swear. But I have no idea how to make women realize that I'm not a creep.

There's nothing I hate more than being viewed as a creep. I consider myself a male feminist. Even though I don't have the guts to stand up for women, I have always wanted to be the kind of guy who would take a woman's side no matter what and call out any guy, even my best friends, if they ever make any misogynistic remarks. I have three sisters, two younger and one older. All four of us were raised by a single mother. So all of the most important people in my life have always been women. I would never do anything as horrible as look up a woman's skirt… Not on purpose, anyway.

I hear others in the room with us. Two more women groan as they come into consciousness.

"What's going on?" one of them asks. "Where are we?"

The girl at the door steps back, moving away from me. She's wearing fuzzy boots too big for her feet, which make a thumping noise as she steps across the floor. The skirt brushes across my nose and tickles me so much that I almost sneeze and give up my act.

"We're locked in!" she cries to the others.

I am finally free to look around, but I decide to keep my eyes closed for a few minutes just so none of them suspect me of being a pervert.

"Where's my phone?"

"I don't have my phone, either."

"How did we get here?"

"The last thing I remember was walking to biology class."

"The last thing I remember was going to my car to get my earpods."

"Well, I was at work waiting for my boyfriend to pick me up."

"Did somebody kidnap us?"

"I don't remember anything."

As I lie here, I try to think back to what happened to me. I was in the cafeteria having a late breakfast and reading a book for literature class. *Animal Farm*. I'd read it before, but the instructor said that we needed to read it three times before class that week. He said you can't understand a book unless you read it at least three times. Not a lot of people were in the cafeteria while I read the book. It was pretty empty. I'm not sure what happened after that. I don't remember going to class or finishing the book. I don't remember even leaving my seat.

I hear movement coming toward me and then feel a boot in my side. The shock of being kicked pops my eyes open. A woman with tattoos, a septum ring, and long black hair is standing over me, staring down at me.

"What do you know?" she asks in an accusatory tone.

I sit up, rubbing the soreness in my side where she kicked me. She didn't kick very hard, just hard enough to wake someone up, but it hurts nonetheless.

"What are we doing here? What happened to us? Do you know anything?"

I just lean back against the wall and shake my head. I don't say anything. There are four women in the room with me, all students from my university. A couple of them seem familiar, but I'm not sure where I've seen them before. Besides the girl with the tattoos, there's a woman with short red hair and an overabundance of makeup, a petite blonde with boobs that seem to be too big for her body and glasses too big for her face, and the panicked girl in the skirt who has long locks of curly brown hair and a dark complexion. They are all incredibly beautiful and not the kind of girls who would ever talk to me.

"What do they want with us?" the girl in the skirt cries, not able to stand still. "I have an exam tomorrow. I need to study or my parents will kill me."

The room is a school classroom, but it doesn't seem to be one I recognize on campus. It feels more like a junior high class, with desks that are so brand new that nobody has ever sat in them long enough to cover them in graffiti or put gum under the seat.

"Does anyone remember how we got here?" I ask them. "I don't remember anything."

The women stare at me, but they don't say anything. They are just as confused as I am.

We introduce ourselves. The girl whose skirt I woke up under is named Madison. The girl with the tattoos who kicked me is Isabella but goes by Bella. The curvy, blonde with glasses is Jennie. And the girl with red hair is Eve.

"I'm Arlo," I tell them.

Madison won't stop pacing around the room. "Is this just a prank? Is somebody messing with us?"

Bella shakes her head. "Would anyone really drug us and put us in this room just to mess with us?"

"Maybe!" Madison cries.

Bella goes to the window and opens the curtain. There is nothing behind it. Just a brick wall. The curtains are just for decoration.

"Would they put us in a place like this if it was just

a prank?" Bella asks the frightened girl. "This isn't a real classroom." She puts her hand against the cold brick wall. "We're probably underground. In a basement." She lifts up a desk with one hand and no effort, as if it's light as cardboard. "These are all just props. Like a movie set."

"Why would they put us in a movie set?" Madison cries.

"We've been kidnapped," Eve says. "They plan to sell us into prostitution overseas."

Madison's face widens in a panic, her eyes ready to erupt into tears. "Prostitution?"

Eve nods. "Yeah. It happens all the time. Don't you watch the news? They get you hooked on drugs like heroin so that you'll be willing to do anything, no matter how depraved, to get your fix."

Madison just collapses against the wall and slides to the floor. "This can't be happening…"

Eve smirks at Madison's reaction. I can't tell if she's serious or just enjoys torturing the frightened girl. She looks like a real bitch. I wouldn't be surprised if she was just saying that to make the other women scared.

Bella is the only one not fazed by Eve's theory. She seems to be the only one in the room who is keeping her cool. "We don't know if that's true. We could have been kidnapped for any number of reasons."

But her words do nothing to calm the others. I wish I could comfort them somehow. There's got to be something I can say. As the only guy in the room, I have to do something to help. Imagining the worst possible reasons for our capture can't be good for us.

I tell them, "If we were kidnapped to be sold into prostitution, why would they kidnap me? I'm a guy. They wouldn't sell me into prostitution."

Eve shakes her head. "Men get sold into prostitution, too." She gets close to me. Her face right in mine. I'm not able to make eye contact. "You're pretty cute. I bet a lot of rich men would want to own you."

I don't have anything to say. I can smell her perfume and see her cleavage poking out of her top. Just being near her is turning me on, and I curse myself for feeling this way, especially in this situation. But most of all, I can't believe she called me *cute*. No girl has ever called me that before. She has to just be fucking with me.

"Or they want to force us to do a porno," Bella says. "If this is a movie set, it makes more sense that's what this is for."

Madison gets even more upset. "I don't want to be in a porno! My parents would disown me!"

When I think about it, I wonder if we really have been kidnapped to perform weird sex acts in front of a camera. The idea disturbs me, but the thought of being able to make love to these four beautiful women doesn't seem like the worst thing in the world. It would be preferable to becoming a sex slave to some rich guy overseas. Though I would never be able to live with myself if I went through with it.

"I'm not saying that's what this is," Bella says. "It's a possibility, but we just need to wait. We'll find out the truth eventually."

I step forward. "Yeah, I think we're jumping to

crazy conclusions. There's got to be a more reasonable explanation. Maybe we've been kidnapped for ransom. Do any of you have rich or influential parents?"

Eve says, "Yeah, my family has money. Do you think that's what they want?"

Bella shakes her head. "My parents are poor as fuck."

"My parents are middle class," Madison says.

"I don't even have parents," Jennie says.

I look down. My family also doesn't have enough money to make me a target. "Well, there's got to be some kind of connection between us. Maybe it's not about the money. Maybe we witnessed something we weren't supposed to. Maybe our parents have something the kidnappers want." I know I'm just grasping at straws, but if we keep talking about it, we might figure out what's going on.

Bella puts her hand on my shoulder and pushes me down into a seat. I'm surprised by how much stronger she is than I am. "It's not worth freaking out over. We don't know a thing. All we're going to do is work ourselves up."

"But we should make a plan," I tell her. "We have to figure out a way to escape, no matter why we've been kidnapped."

"Any ideas?" she asks.

I get up and look around the room. There's only one way in and one way out. I go to the door and kick it. The second my foot connects, a shooting pain rides up my leg. The door is solid metal and doesn't budge an inch. I pick up a desk and throw it at the door, but it just crumples on impact.

"Good job." Eve snickers. "Real effective."

I step back, feeling embarrassed. I don't want to give up, but I have no idea what to do.

"Can we pick the lock?" Madison asks.

Bella looks back. "Have you ever picked a lock before?"

Madison shrugs. It's almost like she assumed Bella would know how to pick a lock because she has tattoos and piercings.

Bella sits down at one of the desks and leans on her elbows. "I think we need to just wait and see what happens. There's no use panicking."

But even as she says this, I can see her hands shaking, her foot tapping anxiously against the floor. She puts up a strong act, but she's just as scared as the rest of us.

An hour passes, and we've become too anxious and exhausted to speak. We all sit at the front of the classroom, leaning against the wall below the whiteboard. The girl with the big boobs, Jennie, sits next to me, rubbing her fingers like there's paint she's trying to peel off. As an art major, I'm always trying to get paint off of my fingers. It gets everywhere and half my clothes are stained in the stuff. My hands are always covered in oils and acrylics; even now pink and purple paint stain my fingernails like nail polish. But Jennie doesn't have anything visible on her hands. She's just rubbing at nothing, too anxious to realize what she's doing.

"Do I know you from somewhere?" I ask her. "You look really familiar. Are you in my anthropology class?"

She looks at me, almost surprised that I've been sitting next to her the whole time.

"Umm..." she begins, straightening the oversized glasses on her face. "No, I don't go to the university. I work at the coffee shop near the campus."

"Oh, maybe that's where I know you from," I say, inching closer. "Lovely Lattes? I do homework there all the time."

"Yeah, that's where I work. But I don't recognize you. Sorry."

She looks away, not very interested in having a conversation. But I don't stop talking. "It's okay. I don't really remember you, either. But I bet that's where I know you from."

I pause for a moment, my gaze shifting to the other women. They are all anxious and unable to speak. I tend to talk when I'm nervous. Nothing makes me more awkward than silence.

"Did you grow up in this town?" I ask her. "I assume you're a local if you don't go to the college."

She shakes her head. "I moved here with some friends. They go to the university. I just came along for the ride because I had nowhere else to go. I can't afford the tuition here and my grades in high school weren't very good, so..."

I feel compelled to keep talking to her. I want to know more about her. It's not normal for me to have the opportunity to talk to a woman and she seems like the least intimidating one to talk to in the room.

"What would you study?" I ask her. "You know, if you could go to the school."

She shrugs. "I don't know. Cosmetology."

On the other side of me, Eve snickers at our conversation and says, "What kind of idiot would go to college for cosmetology?"

Jennie is visibly upset by her words. "I know… But that's the only thing I would be interested in. I'm not good at anything else."

"There's a beauty college in town," I tell her. "My mom went there when I was a kid. It's supposed to be pretty good."

She shakes her head. "I already looked. It's also way too expensive for me. Maybe someday. If I save my money…"

"I'm sure you can do it. I think it's important to follow your dreams. I'm an artist myself and I believe—"

She cuts me off. "I'm sorry. I have a boyfriend. I'm not interested… especially right now."

I look at her with shock in my eyes. Did she think I was interested in her sexually? I was just trying to have a conversation.

"No, I didn't mean it like that…" I try to explain.

Bella laughs and yells, "Shot down!"

I snap at her. "I wasn't hitting on her. I don't do that."

Eve rolls her eyes. "Yeah, right…"

"I was just trying to break the silence," I tell them.

But they don't listen to me. I'm a guy, after all. They must be used to guys who have no interest in talking to women for any reason but to get in their pants.

Before I defend myself further, a man's voice fills the classroom. He clears his throat. A tapping sound follows, then feedback squeals, making everyone wince. I look up, searching for a speaker or some visible sign of where the voice is coming from.

"Hello, is this on?" the person asks.

He sounds young, not much older than us. My first thought is that Madison was right. This has to be a prank. As he speaks, there's a laugh behind his voice, something excited and giddy. He must be the one who brought us here just to mess with us.

"Attention all students. This is Principal Games speaking. I'm sure you're all curious about how you got here and why you've been brought here today. I trust you're anxious to see what's in store for you."

The announcer guy chuckles, his voice pulling away from the microphone. He sounds like a frat boy, surrounded by his friends who also think this is all very funny. But to the five people in this room, none of this is funny at all.

Madison stands up and cries, "Let us out of here! We want to go home!"

Principal Games just chuckles in response, but then composes himself. He tries to sound as serious as he possibly can. As if the words he wants to say are very important and not to be taken lightly at all.

"I'm sorry, Madison," the Principal says. "But you can't leave just yet."

The five of us go quiet. We're surprised that the man

answered us back. This announcement isn't being broadcast across an entire school. It is only for the sake of the people in this room. And they are able to hear us as we speak. Looking closely at the ceiling, I wonder if we are being filmed. We must be surrounded by cameras. This guy has been watching us the whole time.

Principal Games continues:

"I've brought you all here to play a game. The name of the game is Kiss, Fuck, Marry, Kill. I have chosen the five of you and brought you here to play this for me. There is one man and four women. How the game works is that the man will choose between the four women. He gets to decide which one he gets to kiss, which one he gets to fuck, which one he gets to marry, and which one he gets to kill."

I almost laugh after he says this, but I bite my tongue. It seems so ridiculous that it can't possibly be true.

"You can't be serious," Eve says.

Madison looks at the rest of us, ready to have a panic attack.

"Is this a joke? This has to be a joke." She turns to the rest of us. "Right?"

"This isn't a joke," Principal Games tells us. "We have taken you far away from civilization and placed you in an underground facility. There is no escape. Nobody knows you're here. No help will ever come. The room you are in is sealed tight enough to survive a nuclear blast. You have no choice but to play the game."

Eve stands up and flips off the fire alarm as though she thinks that's where the camera must be. "Fuck off, loser. Do you think we'd actually believe this bullshit?" She goes to the door and wiggles the handle, kicking it and trying to force her way through. "Let me the fuck out of here."

Principal Games just laughs. "Sorry, babe, but this is really happening. We're not letting you out until the game's over."

"What happens if we refuse?" Bella asks.

Principal Games lets out a sigh. "Well, you wouldn't want to do that, Isabella. If you refuse to play the game or fail to execute each of the challenges, then all five of you will be killed."

"Bullshit," Eve yells. "Just fucking try to kill me and see what happens to you. Do you know who my father is? He will hunt your ass down Liam Neeson style if anything happens to me."

Principal Games laughs at her threat. "We're very well aware of who your father is, Eve. He might be rich, resourceful, and dangerous to any ordinary person. But my employers are far more dangerous than he is. He doesn't frighten us."

A monitor descends from a slit in the ceiling. When we see it moving, we all direct our attention to it.

Eve steps away from the door and moves closer. "What the hell is this?"

"It seems you need proof of the situation you're in," says Principal Games.

A video appears on the screen. There are five people standing in the same room we are, all the same age as us. They look just as confused and scared as we do.

One man and four women. There's no audio. Then the clip cuts to a scene of the man having sex with one of the women. It cuts quickly to another clip of the man breaking a woman's neck and dropping her body to the floor as the other women hold each other, crying.

"And here's what happened to the last contestants who refused to play the game."

A new video shows a different five people in the classroom. They are screaming and yelling, banging on the door. The room is flooded with gas and all five of them slowly fall to the ground and lose consciousness. Two men enter the room dressed in black with handguns and skiing masks over their faces. They go to each of the contestants and put bullets in their heads one at a time. Then a cleanup crew comes in and covers them in plastic. The video ends.

"Do you believe me now?" Principal Games asks. "The situation you're in is real. Some very powerful people are paying a lot of money for you to put on a show for them. And we expect you to play. Whether you like it or not."

As the screen ascends back into the ceiling, the four women go quiet. No one speaks. No one moves. Their eyes dart between each other, then to the floor, then back again. Fists clench. Jaws tighten. But there's no denying it. This is real. We have no choice but to play the game.

CHAPTER TWO

Although the women are in a panic, I don't know how to feel about the situation. It is horrific. It is detestable. But I am safe. No matter what happens, as long as I play the game, I will survive. Most people in this situation would see me as the lucky one. Nothing bad will happen to me. But how can I live with myself if I go through with it? Why do I have to be responsible for the horrible things that are about to happen to these women? The thought makes me sick. I feel so guilty about it that I can hardly breathe. I can't do it. I can't just pick and choose which one to fuck or kill. What kind of person would that make me?

I know several guys who would love to be in the position I'm in. My dorm roommate is one of them. If he could force a woman to have sex with him upon penalty of death, he would be overjoyed. And being able to kill a woman who was ugly or fat or was a bitch to him? He would love that, too. He always talks about killing bitches who have turned him down whenever they made him feel like a loser for hitting on them. That guy was born for a game like this. But I wish a guy like him were on the other side. If he were the one who was to be killed because he didn't meet a woman's standards, he wouldn't see the fun in that at all. Personally, I think I would rather be on the side of the women. I wish a woman were choosing between me and three other men. Even if I were the one who was chosen to be killed, at least I wouldn't have to kill someone. At least I wouldn't have to bear the weight of deciding which one has to die and which one has to be forced to have sex with me.

I get to my feet, my whole body trembling. Everyone looks at me, almost as though they forgot I was here. They look at me with disgust, as though they think I'm in on all this for some reason. Or maybe they're just pissed at me for being in the position to choose between them. Either way, I'm feeling completely alone in this situation. Not a single person is on my side. Not a single one feels empathy for me. I don't blame them, but I wish they would understand what it's like to be in my shoes.

"I can't do this," I tell the fire alarm, walking toward what I believe is the camera. "I won't choose. It isn't fair."

"If you don't choose, Arlo, then all of you will die," Principal Games tells me over the intercom.

I hesitate for a moment, not sure what to say. I know I can't refuse to do anything, but there has to be a way to make a choice that is morally acceptable to me.

After a moment of thought, I say, "Then I choose me to be the one who is killed. I won't kill any of these women. If anyone has to die, I'd rather it be me."

When I glance at the women, their expressions haven't

changed. They still look at me with disgust, not buying a word of it. As if I'm only offering to sacrifice myself to make them like me. As though I don't mean a word of it.

Only Madison believes that I'm genuine and agrees with the arrangement. She exclaims, "Yeah, let him be the one to die. Let the rest of us go."

But Principal Games sighs into the intercom and says, "That's against the rules. You can't choose yourself, Arlo. You can't kiss, fuck, marry, or kill yourself. If you try to do any of these, then all five of you will die. If you kill yourself or if any of the women decide to kill you, it will be game over. None of you will survive."

I look down, not sure what else to say. I really don't want to kill myself, even though I said that I would. If I had to choose between who gets to live and who gets to die, I would definitely sacrifice myself for any of these women, even if they hate me. But I don't really want to give up my life here. I wish this wasn't happening to me.

"So which will you choose, Arlo?" asks Principal Games. "Which one will you kiss, which one will you fuck, which one will you marry, and which one will you kill?"

I take a deep breath and shake my head. "I have no idea..."

Eve yells at me, "You're not fucking me, loser!"

Bella laughs at her outburst. "Then he can kill you."

Eve's eyes light up with anger at the other woman. "No way, he wouldn't ever choose me as kill. I'm too hot."

"But you're a bitch," Bella says. "Why wouldn't he choose you as kill?"

"I'm not a bitch!" Eve cries.

"You've been a bitch since you got here. Let's face it. You're a bitch, I kicked him in the stomach, Jennie shot him down and Madison is obnoxious. He has reasons to choose any one of us as kill."

Madison's eyes widen. "I'm not obnoxious!" Then she looks at me. "You wouldn't kill me, would you? I haven't been mean to you!"

Bella snickers. "You just enthusiastically agreed that he should die to save yourself. You really think he sees you as nice after that?"

"I didn't mean it like that!" Madison approaches me. "You know I didn't want you to die, right? I'm not a horrible person. Please don't choose me as kill!"

I don't know how to respond to her. I just lower my eyes and step back. I say, "No, of course I won't choose you. I'm not an asshole."

"Then who are you going to choose?" Eve asks.

I shrug. "I don't know…"

"Well, you have to choose, Arlo," says Principal Games. "You have two hours to make your first choice. If you haven't made a single choice by then, it's game over for all of you."

I look at the women and can't handle the sight of them. They have so much anguish in their eyes. I wish I could do something to comfort them but I'm probably the last person they'd want that from now.

"And if I make my choices, we'll all be allowed to leave? You'll let us go?"

Principal Games responds, "Yes, outside of the woman

who is killed, the rest of you will be able to go home. As long as you say nothing about what has happened to you here today, you will be free to continue your lives like normal."

It's easy for him to say. There's no way I can live a normal life if I do what he wants me to do.

Bella gets up and speaks to the camera.

She asks, "How does *marry* even work, anyway? Does he just have to sign a marriage certificate? Could he just get a divorce immediately after we leave, or are you going to force him to stay married somehow?"

"Excellent question, Isabella!" says Principal Games. "Whoever Arlo chooses to marry, they will be expected to stay together until death do they part. That means they must move in together, sleep in the same bed, and even have at least one child together within the next ten years. They will be monitored by our people so they won't be allowed to cheat. If they ever spend more than ten days apart, then punishment will fall on all of you. You all will most likely be put to death. So it would be in the best interest of all of you to follow the rules. The marriage choice is probably the most difficult decision to make. It will be something you'll be stuck with for the rest of your life. Make sure to choose wisely, Arlo. The woman of your future is in this room with you right now."

I look at the women. Not a single one of them looks like they want me to choose them for marriage. Whoever I end up deciding on, they will likely be miserable for the rest of their lives.

"It's time to make a decision, Arlo," Principal Games says.

An hour has passed, and I have just been trying to find a way out of this. I haven't given much thought to who I will kiss, fuck, marry, or kill. I keep thinking someone will come and save us. I keep thinking there's got to be a way for us to escape. There's a part of me that still thinks this could be an elaborate prank, but just in case it's not, I still have to play the game. If it is a joke, they'll stop me before I have to kill, won't they? Maybe even before I have to fuck. I really hope this is just a prank. I really can't go through with any of the options before me.

The women are lined up on one end of the room, as Principal Games instructed them. They all just stand there like contestants in a game, while I stand on the other side of the room, trying to figure out what I should do.

"I can't decide..." I tell them. "I'm sorry. It's too much for me."

But this only angers the women more.

"You have to," Bella tells me. "If you don't choose, then we're all going to die."

"Then you should choose," I tell them. "Which one of you wants to kiss me, marry me, or fuck me? I'll choose whoever wants to be chosen."

But it isn't as easy as that. None of them wants to be chosen for any of those. They don't want to decide any more than I do. They hate that I gave them the option of choosing for me.

"What about kill?" I asked them. "Are any of you willing to sacrifice yourself to save the others?"

They look at each other, but none of them speaks. Not a single one of them is willing to die voluntarily, even to save the others. Maybe if they were friends, it would be a different story. But they're all strangers. They have no interest in dying for strangers.

I get frustrated. "Come on. Please help me. One of you has to be willing to do one of them. What about kiss? Won't even one of you be willing to kiss me?"

But the women don't respond. Not a single one even wants to kiss me. Am I that repulsive? I might not be the most handsome guy on campus, but I'm not the ugliest either. Why won't a single one of them agree to do even such a little thing as kiss me? It is a huge blow to my ego. I never knew I was that repulsive. They would rather die than kiss me? Or are they just scared? Do they think kissing me would mean they have to accept the situation they're in? I just don't get it.

While I shake uncontrollably, feeling rejected and confused, Bella steps forward.

"If you're letting us decide, I'll kiss you," she says.

"Really?" I ask.

Bella shrugs. "Sure. Why not?"

Bella approaches me. She doesn't hesitate. She wraps her arms around me and kisses me deeply. Her pierced tongue enters my mouth and explores like she actually means it. The metal piercing clacks against my teeth as she presses herself close to me. I feel her breasts against my body, and I instantly fall in love. I've never had a girlfriend. I've never kissed a girl before. For a second, I'm able to forget all about the situation we're in and just enjoy the moment. I wish she wasn't doing it because she was forced to. I wish she were kissing me for real, because she really liked me. I wish I had a girlfriend as beautiful and confident as her.

When she pulls away, I feel disappointed, as though I wish it would continue for as long as possible. My eyes are still closed as a strand of saliva connects our mouths. My penis becomes erect, and I'm not able to cover it before the other girls notice. The three on the other side of the room look on with disgust. They probably can't believe I'm such a creep. They probably can't believe Bella would actually kiss a guy like me.

Bella steps away and turns to the fire alarm. "Was that good enough or should I continue?"

I so wish she would continue.

But Principal Games is satisfied with the kiss. "Good job, you two. The first decision has been made. Bella has passed the first round. She gets to survive."

The other girls freak out as Bella steps to the side of the room, proud of herself. She doesn't even look at the other women, not wanting to witness their jealousy for not deciding before her. She knows that she made the right call. Every single one of them would have preferred kiss over the other options, but they didn't realize it until it was too late.

"No fair!" Madison cries.

"Why did you get kiss?" Eve yells. "He should have kissed me!"

Bella just shrugs. "He let us decide. I just took him up on the offer."

"You bitch," Eve says.

But Bella isn't fazed by their outbursts. She's the luckiest of us and she knows it. Even though I'm in the place of power, I'm going to be forced to marry someone who doesn't love me, not to mention living with the guilt of everything that I'll do. I personally wish I were in her shoes. Of all of them, I'm happy she was chosen for kiss. She will be the only one who's able to sleep well after today.

"One down, three to go," says Principal Games. "You have two more hours to make your next selection, Arlo. But it's only going to get harder from here. Are you really going to have the women decide which one of them fucks you, marries you, or is killed by you? You'll have to make the decision yourself sooner or later."

His words hit me pretty hard. I really do want to get through this game without making another decision.

"Why don't you take an hour or so to think about it?" Principal Games says. "I'm sure it's not an easy choice for someone like you. You're a virgin, aren't you? Did you ever think your first time would be in a place like this?" He laughs loudly into the microphone. "Get ready. You're about to have the ride of your life."

Principal Games goes quiet after that and I'm left to

my own thoughts. The other girls don't look at me. They cower on the other side of the room, thinking I'm the worst man they've ever met. Not a single one of them wants to know who I will choose. They hate me for even being given the choice in the first place. I have no idea what I'm going to do.

I sit down at a desk and put my face in my hands. After a few minutes, Bella comes to me and sits at a desk next to mine.

She says, "I know it's hard, but you're going to have to make a choice eventually. Don't feel guilty. It's not your fault we're here."

When she says this, my eyes light up. I can't tell if she is actually empathizing with me or if she just wants to give me the strength to make a decision so that she doesn't die.

"I don't know how to choose," I tell her. "I don't want to do it."

Bella tries to help. "Well, forget this game is real. If you were playing this for fun with your friends, which woman would you choose for fuck, marry, and kill?"

I shake my head. "I would never play such a sexist game with my friends."

Bella isn't happy with my response. "Fuck that. Who cares if it's sexist? Just tell me who you'd choose? You don't have to pick them. Just pretend there's no consequence to your decision."

I shrug. I know that making any decision at all would make me a horrible person. But she's looking at me with such a serious face that I feel like I can't just refuse to give her an answer.

"Well, I would choose Eve as either fuck or kill. I wouldn't marry her. She seems like she would be a nightmare. Jennie I would choose for fuck or marry, I guess. Madison maybe marry. I couldn't choose kill for any of them, though. I don't want any of them to die."

"But you said you'd choose Eve as fuck or kill?" Bella asks. "Why not make her kill? She's a total bitch, isn't she?"

"But I don't want her to die…"

Bella shrugs. "Yeah, but would you rather the other two die? You said Eve is fuck or kill, so you should kill her. Jennie is fuck or marry, so you should fuck her. And Madison you said you'd marry, so marry her. It's a simple choice, isn't it? Just do that. It sucks, I know. But it's an easy choice."

I look down. I'm not sure I can agree with that decision, but I don't deny that it would be an okay answer.

As we speak, the other girls hear bits and pieces of the conversation, but they don't exactly get what was said.

"What are you two talking about?" Eve asks. "You better not be trying to make a decision for him, Bella."

"I'm just trying to make sure he doesn't wimp out," Bella says.

"You told him to kill me, didn't you?" Eve asks. She looks at me. "You better not kill me, asshole! If you try to kill me, I'll fucking kill myself first, and then you'll all be fucked."

"Well, if you kill yourself, then the problem will be solved, won't it?"

"Fuck no! He has to kill someone himself." She turns to the fire alarm. "Tell them, you assholes! He has to kill someone himself, doesn't he?"

Principal Games comes on the intercom. He's obviously been listening the whole time.

"Yes, if somebody kills themselves, then that can't be considered a kill. He can, however, fuck or marry someone already dead. In fact, choosing to marry someone who is already dead would work out well for Arlo because he won't actually have to spend his life with them. The rule is till death do you part, so if the woman is already dead, then they don't have to stay together. Wouldn't that be great, Arlo? Maybe you should encourage one of them to kill themselves."

His words do not give me any comfort. I would not be happy if any of them killed themselves, and I'd still be forced to kill another one. I really hope Eve isn't serious about what she plans to do.

I turn to Bella. Tears are beginning to form in my eyes. "I really don't think I can kill anyone."

She gets up and puts her hands on my shoulders, as though she is planning to give me a massage, but she only squeezes them.

"You've got to be strong," she tells me. "All of our lives depend on you. Don't ruin this for us. All you have to do is follow your gut. Kill Eve, fuck Jennie, marry Madison. Then we can all go home."

I listen to her, thinking about whether I should actually make that decision. But as she leans in and caresses my cheek, pressing her face against my neck, I realize that she is really just interested in saving herself. She doesn't care about me or the other women one bit.

CHAPTER THREE

When I was a kid, my sisters used to like to dress me up like a girl. They put me in one of their dresses and placed a black Halloween wig over my short hair. They would apply makeup to me and tell me how pretty I would look if I were a girl. Then they would pretend that I was one of them, a fourth sister, and take me out to the mall to see if anyone would notice. They would address me as Arla instead of Arlo and act like I've never been their brother at all.

I didn't have a father or brothers to stop them or to criticize me for letting them do it to me. And because there were three of them, I was outnumbered and not really able to resist. A part of me didn't want to resist, to be honest. I kind of liked it when they would dress me up. Not because I wanted to be a girl, but because I liked the attention. My sisters never really accepted me because I was a boy. I always felt like an outcast, that I didn't belong. I had vagina-envy, if that's a thing. So by being dressed up as a girl, I felt like I finally belonged. Like I was part of the sisterhood. It was the only time I ever really felt close to them.

But it didn't go on for too long. Just a year or two. Even after some kids at my school saw me hanging out in girls' clothing and made fun of me ruthlessly, I was still okay with being dressed up. What ended it was when I went through puberty. I became more masculine and bulky. My sisters no longer thought I looked pretty when they dressed me up. They thought I looked gross. So they didn't do it anymore. They no longer invited me to hang out with them. They no longer accepted me as one of the sisters. And I was alone again. Just a guy in a household of women who wanted nothing to do with me other than complain about how I left the toilet seat up or masturbated too much to online porn when I thought everyone was asleep. I became just another disgusting perverted man in their eyes. It was like Arla never existed. And every day I became more and more disgusted by who and what I was.

Now that I'm in this situation, I'm sure my sisters would hate me even more. The fact that I'm playing this game, even if it was for the sake of saving most of our lives, they would disown me. They wouldn't let me come home for the holidays or invite me to their weddings. They wouldn't see me as even their gross brother anymore. They would just see me as a piece of trash, like all the other guys they know.

Now that I have to make my next decision, I don't know what I'm going to do. I can't help but see these women as my sisters. Even though they hate me, I love my sisters and look up to them. If they were put in this situation, I would want to kill every single person responsible. And I would want to kill the man who chose their fate more than anyone. Even if he was forced into the position, like me, I couldn't handle the thought of a guy having sex with one of my sisters against their will, forcing one to marry him, or killing one of them. I just couldn't let him live. I'm sure the families of all these women will feel the same way about me.

Bella comes up to me and places her hand on my shoulder.

"It's time," she says. "You have to make your next choice."

I look at her with terror in my eyes. I had well over an hour to think about it, but my thoughts only made it more difficult. The decision was hard before, but now it's impossible. I can't make a choice.

She glares at me with a serious expression, telling me that I better decide or she's going to kick my ass. But I just shake my head and say, "I don't know…"

The three girls stand there, waiting. All of them are very tense, visibly shaking, dreading what is about to come next. Eve can't handle the pressure and explodes.

She goes to the fire alarm, presuming it's the camera, and yells, "You motherfuckers! I'm going to fucking kill every one of you. Do you here that? When I get out of here, I'm going to make all of you pay. I promise you that!"

The man on the intercom laughs at her.

"Do you really think you're getting out of this alive?" asks Principal Games. "We have a betting pool going up here and everyone thinks that you're going to be the one he chooses for kill. I highly doubt you're going to make the cut."

"Fuck that!" Eve says. She turns to me. "You won't choose me as kill, will you, Arlo? Choose one of the ugly bitches over there. Let me live so I can kill these assholes."

I look at the other women. Both of them are getting even more upset. Madison wants to speak up, attempting to defend herself, argue that she should be the one to be saved instead of Eve. But Madison can't speak. She just opens her mouth and nothing but whimpers come out.

Eve steps away from the camera. "Fuck it. Choose me as fuck." She comes to me. "I've fucked uglier guys than you. I might have been drunk, but under the circumstances I don't have a choice. I'd rather fuck you than die or marry you. So pick me."

I feel bad that she's seeing me as an ugly guy she would need to be drunk to sleep with. She had called me cute earlier. I thought there must have been at least a little truth to that. Maybe she changed her mind once she learned about the rules of the game and what my role would be. Any cute factor I had would have been lost instantly the second I was put in a place of power. But she does say she's willing to be chosen as the one who has sex with me. There's got to be something to that, isn't there?

Bella whispers in my ear, "This isn't part of the plan. Don't pick her."

Eve pushes Bella back. "You're out of this game, bitch. Get the fuck back." Then she gets really close to me, pressing her body against mine. I can feel her padded bra poking me in the chest through her shirt. "Come on. Fuck me. Show me what you've got." Then she grabs my ass, and I immediately become erect.

"Okay…" I say, not able to resist her. I've never been touched like this by a woman before. I feel weak to her advances. There's no way I couldn't choose her when she actually offers herself like this.

Bella whips around, disgusted by the display. "Jesus fuck." She goes back to the corner and sits down, flashing me an annoyed expression. She really wanted me to choose Eve as kill.

"Let's do it," Eve tells me. "Let's get this over with so that we can go home."

Then she unzips my pants and pulls them down to my ankles.

"You have thirty minutes to get the job done," says Principal Games. "Arlo needs to fully release, or it doesn't count. If he doesn't cum by the end of the timer, then you all die."

When he says this, both Eve and I freak out. She looks at me with an annoyed expression. "You better fucking cum. If we do this and I die anyway, I'm going to be so fucking pissed."

But after she says this and after being given a time limit, the pressure hits me way too hard. My penis instantly deflates and I become too afraid to have sex.

Eve strips off her clothes in front of everyone as though it were the most normal thing in the world. When she takes off her bra, my eyes lock on her breasts. They are small but perky. Her areolas are small, but her nipples are long and erect. I can't take my eyes off them. I've been to a strip club once and did figure painting in art class with live nude models, so I've seen naked women in person before. But I've never felt this way after seeing a naked woman in my life.

But as I stand here ogling her body, Eve becomes irritated with me for being too shy to get naked with her.

"Do I have to do everything myself?" she asks.

She takes off my shirt and shoes, and then my underwear. One of her nipples brushes against my arm as she undresses me, and I blush. I stand naked in front of the women, wearing only my socks. I quickly cover my penis, ashamed of my body. I've never had sex with anyone before. I never thought my first time would be such a horrible experience.

"Come on, let's do this," Eve says. She pulls my hands from my penis and then groans with frustration. "Limp dick motherfucker. You better get hard."

She grabs my penis and then begins to stroke it, but it doesn't get hard.

"Eww… it's so gross. You've got more foreskin than penis."

Eve keeps stroking, but it doesn't react. I'm too

embarrassed and horrified to get an erection.

"I've never seen a penis as small as yours. Are you sure you're a man? You're more like a woman with a big clit."

Bella groans and puts her hands on her face. "Jesus Christ… Are you stupid or what? He's never going to be able to get it up if you insult him like that."

Eve looks over at her. "You try to fuck him then. Put his gross, shriveled-up dick in you and see how you like it."

"Twenty minutes," Principal Games says.

Eve shrieks in frustration. "Fuck!"

She gets down on the floor and pulls me on top of her. Then she fingers herself to get herself wet with one hand while rubbing my penis against her labia. I mostly just feel her itchy pubic hair scratching against my foreskin. The sensation is far more awkward than pleasurable. I can't believe this is happening. I feel like such a scumbag. I also feel pathetic and humiliated. If I'd known sex would be like this, then I'd rather never have it at all. I never want to go through anything like this ever again.

Eve glares at me with more hate than I've ever seen. "Just get hard, asshole. What the hell is wrong with you?"

"I'm sorry…" I tell her. "I've never done this before."

"Fucking loser," she says, letting go of my penis. "This is impossible."

When she sees Eve giving up, Bella gets to her feet.

"Let me do it," Bella tells her. "You're going to get us all killed."

I tense up when Bella comes behind me and wraps

her arms around me.

She whispers into my ear. "Just ignore her. Focus on me."

Out of nowhere, Bella starts kissing my neck. She licks me from my jaw to my mouth and then kisses me deeply, even more passionately than before. I know she's only doing it to save herself, but I let myself fall into the fantasy that she actually likes me. She removes her shirt and bra and presses her breasts against my back. Then she grabs my dick and strokes it slowly. She's not impatient or insulting like Eve. I really wish I were strong enough to make a decision myself so I could have chosen her for this role. I wouldn't want to force this on her, but it would have been so much better with someone like her.

"What the fuck, bitch?" Eve yells. "Back the fuck off."

"Just lie there and wait," Bella tells her.

As Bella jerks me off until I become erect, the principal comes onto the intercom system.

"Holy shit!" he yells. "This is a first! We've never seen two women at the same time. Aren't you lucky, Arlo? You should be thanking the gods we chose you to play this game."

His words disgust me so much that my erection dies a little. There's nothing good about being in this situation. I will loathe them for the rest of my life for choosing me. And the guilt of this moment will be with me for the rest of my life.

Bella tries to get me back in the mood. "Just ignore him. Ignore everyone. Just focus on me."

I try to do as she says. Her breasts pressing against

my back feel so amazing. I wish I could see them. I wish I could touch them. I wish I could make love to her with every fiber of my being. But once I become erect, she guides me into Eve.

As I feel my penis inserted, Eve shrieks and pulls back. Bella grabs her by the thigh, trying to pull her back.

"Don't fuck this up for us," Bella tells Eve.

Eve cringes at us, a look of disgust on her face. "I can't help it. This is too fucked up."

"Just don't be quiet and don't move."

Bella continues to kiss me as she pushes me into Eve, forcing me deeper into the girl that hates me more than anyone right now. I'm disgusted with myself, but I can't help but continue.

"Ten more minutes," Principal Games says. "No, actually… Eight more minutes. Sorry about that. Hurry up if you all want to survive. You don't want this all to be for nothing, do you?"

Bella looks over at the camera, "Shut up, asshole!"

Then she goes to me. "Ignore the time. Just focus. You're almost there."

Bella grabs my ass and brushes my hair out of my eyes. Then Eve pushes her away.

"Back off," Eve tells her. "I've got this."

Then Eve grabs me and pulls me close to her. I'm able to have sex with Eve without Bella's help. I feel as though training wheels have been taken off, and I'm able to ride a bike on my own. I still feel disgusted with myself, but I try to bury my thoughts and focus on the task at hand. I can't think about how horrible this is for

Eve. I can't think about the other two women who await their own fate. I just have to get this over with so that we aren't all killed on the spot.

When I cum, Eve cries out. Not in pleasure. She cries as though my sperm is poison to her body. She claws my back, digging her nails into my skin in order to hurt me as much as she can, getting her frustration out on me for doing this to her. Then she pushes me off of her and grabs her clothes. She leaves her bra on the floor and pulls on her shirt, just to cover herself as quickly as she can.

"Did he cum?" Principal Games asks. "We couldn't tell. We need proof."

Eve reaches between her legs and pulls out a glob of my spunk. Then she goes to the fire alarm and smears it across what she thinks is the camera lens.

"Is that proof enough for you, asshole?"

Then she puts her underwear and pants back on. She looks more pissed off then anyone I've ever seen before.

"Please clean that off," says Principal Games. "Our clients need to be able to see what happens next."

Eve grunts and uses her bra to clean off the camera lens. Then she tosses it aside.

I slowly put my clothes back on, feeling like I want to cry. I know that Eve was in a worse situation than I was, but I feel like such a creep and a loser. I feel traumatized. It was the worst experience in my entire life. I can't believe I actually went through with it.

After she puts her shirt back on, Bella comes closer and tries to comfort me. "You did good, Arlo. At least some of us will survive now." She looks over at Eve who seems ready to kill someone. "But I still think you made the wrong choice. It's going to be a lot harder to make your choices now. I don't think I could choose which of the remaining two will have to die."

I look over at Madison and Jennie. They are so frightened they can't even speak. They know that the worst two options are left. One of them will die. One of them will have to spend the rest of her life with me. Maybe I did make the wrong decision. Maybe I should have let Eve be the one to die.

As Eve moves to the side of the room, no longer a contestant in the game, she looks at me with repulsion and says, "Don't go telling anyone on campus that you fucked me. That was basically rape. It doesn't count."

I just find myself nodding my head. There's no way I would tell anyone about that. Nobody would believe me anyway.

CHAPTER FOUR

"Two down and two to go," says Principal Games. "Only marry and kill left. It's all up to you, Arlo. Which one of these fine ladies are you interested in spending the rest of your life with, and which one are you going to put to death? Only you can decide. Think carefully. You have two more hours to make your final decision. If you wimp out, then all of this will be for nothing. You will die having had the most pathetic excuse for lovemaking that I've ever seen in my life, and still got everyone in the room killed. So whatever option you go with, make sure to make a choice. It will be bad for all of you if you can't go through with it."

As I stand here, looking at the two frightened women, I realize that I made a horrible decision. I left the two nicest, most innocent girls for the two most horrible choices. I wish I had chosen Bella for marry and Eve for kill. Not that I want Eve to die or force Bella to marry me, but I just think the two remaining are the ones who deserve this the least. They are so pretty and smart and better than me. I don't belong in this position. I wish I were back at my dorm with my douchebag roommate, talking about all the girls that he plans to have sex with. I used to think my roommate was the most toxic male I've ever met, but now I feel like I'm far worse than he is. He's never actually forced a woman to have sex with him before. He's never killed anyone. I'm just a horrible person, and I'll loathe myself for the rest of my life.

"Come on, Arlo," Eve tells me. "Choose one of them. Don't fuck this up for the rest of us."

I look at her. She seems like she's completely over the experience we just had, like she's already blocked it out of her memory.

"I can't choose who lives and who dies," I tell her.

"Just flip a coin," Eve says. "Who cares? At least we'll survive."

I shake my head, blocking her out. I don't have a coin anyway. I don't think I can leave this up to a coin flip even if I had one. The only choice I have is to do what I've done until now. I have to let them decide. I know it's a cowardly move, but I don't want the weight of such a decision on me.

Before I know it, I'm asking them, "Do either of you want to marry me? I know it's horrible, but I don't know who to choose. If either of you wants to marry me, I'll choose you. I don't care which one. I think you both seem really nice."

Madison breaks through her nerves and speaks up. "I don't want to die! Please don't choose for me to die."

"Then do you want me to marry you?" I ask.

She goes quiet and looks away, not willing to give

me a response.

"Just don't kill me..." she says.

I look at Jennie. She's been mostly silent this whole time. She has just been standing there, not willing to speak up for herself. I don't want her to die. Even though she reacted to me like I was hitting on her, I still think she's a worthwhile person who doesn't deserve to be in this situation. Neither of them does.

"Stop dicking around and choose one," Eve says.

Bella pushes her. "He has time. Don't rush him."

I look at Jennie. "What about you? Would you marry me?"

She glowers at me and then shakes her head. "I already have a boyfriend. I'm in love with him." She looks at Madison and then back at me. "I am unwilling to kiss, fuck, or marry you unless you force me to. I love my boyfriend too much. We were planning to get married after he finishes school. I couldn't do that to him. If you ask me to marry you, then I'll say no. If you choose to kill me, then I'll accept it. But I refuse to play this game. I won't be your wife."

I'm shocked by her resolve. None of the rest of us were willing to die. None of us could just refuse to play because it went against our values. She is the only one who is strong enough to say no, even if it means her death.

"So you want me to choose you for kill instead of marry?" I ask her.

She shrugs. "I don't know. Choose whoever you want. But if you choose me for marry, I will never love you. Even if we are forced to live with each other and sleep in the same bed, I will never see you as my husband. I will always love my boyfriend. He is the only one I want to be with. It's either him or no one."

I don't know how to take that. She's basically telling me not to choose her for marry. But I can't just choose her for kill, even if she refuses to marry me.

"Just kill her," Eve says. "Then we can all go home."

I think about it for a moment. Madison seems desperate to stay alive. Of anyone, she's the one who wants to live the most. I can't choose to kill her. But Jennie can't die either.

"What about your dream?" I ask Jennie. "You said you wanted to get into cosmetology. Do you really want to die before that? Is your boyfriend worth more than that?"

Jennie shrugs again. "I care more about him than anything. You wouldn't understand. He accepts me for who I am. He loves me no matter how stupid I am or how worthless I am as a human being. I could never betray him. I'd rather die than do that."

I'm shocked to hear her say that. I wasn't expecting it. I wish I were with a girl like her. I wish I had somebody who loved me so much that they'd rather die than betray me. Thinking about it, I start to feel envious of her boyfriend. Why couldn't I be with a girl like her? Why does no girl want to date me or even be friends with me? She is the best woman in this room, and she deserves so much more than being forced to play this horrible game.

"Just kill me," Jennie says. "I don't want Madison to die. Choose her for marry and me for kill. I'm okay with that. I'd rather not have her death on my conscience."

Madison's eyes widen in shock, disturbed by the idea of marrying me. But then she quickly changes her mind. She looks at me with pleading eyes. "I'll marry you. If she's okay with dying, then I'm okay with being your wife. Just please don't kill me. I want to live. I'll be the best wife in the world. I'll do anything you want. Please choose to marry me."

I look at Madison. Tears are in her eyes. She seems serious. She really will do anything to survive. When I look at Jennie, I only see the dead look of somebody who's already decided her fate. The decision is clear. I only have to make my choice. But the words don't come out of my mouth. I step away from them, moving to the other side of the room. This is too hard. No matter who I choose, I'll have to kill one of them. I don't have it in me. I'd rather die than have to kill either of them.

I let the time pass on the clock, unwilling to budge. Eve and Bella urge me to make a decision, but I block them out. I don't want anyone to die, but if the people holding us here decide to kill us, at least the blood won't be on my hands. It will be their sin, not mine. Maybe it would be better if I just let everyone die. I'm not strong enough to kill someone to save the rest of us. I wonder if this is just a joke. Maybe we are just being tested to see how far we go. If I do nothing, maybe they will just let us go. Maybe they will kill all of us if I make the wrong decision. Maybe they will kill all of us even if I do play the game all the way to the end. This way, I can die knowing that I wasn't a murderer. This way, I can die feeling that I did the right thing.

"It's time, Arlo," says Principal Games. "You have to make your decision. Which one will you marry? Which one will you kill? The decision is yours and yours alone."

I just shake my head, unwilling to answer.

Eve and Bella freak out on me.

"Come on, asshole!" Eve cries. "Why are you hesitating? Just kill Jennie and marry Madison. Don't be such a loser."

I just shake her words off and ignore her. Then Bella comes forward.

"Listen, Arlo. Our lives are in your hands. I know it's hard, but you have to decide. Don't just let us die. I know it's horrible, but don't take the weight of murdering somebody all on yourself. It's not your fault. You won't be murdering anyone. It's them." She points to the camera. "They are the ones killing her. And we're just as guilty as you for egging you on. So don't think it all lies on you. You can do this. Just decide."

I let out a sigh and shake my head. "I can't do it," I tell them. "I can't kill another person, especially not one of them."

Jennie and Madison both remind me of my two younger sisters. My youngest sister is so much like Jennie. Quiet, strong, humble, takes no shit from anyone. And Madison is like my other younger sister. Emotional, nervous, cute, nice, wears her heart on her sleeve. I couldn't possibly harm either one of them.

Principal Games says, "Don't give up now, Arlo. You're so close to the finish line."

I look at Jennie and Madison. I don't want them to die. Even if they plan to kill all of us after this, there's still a chance that they are telling the truth. I can't just let everyone die if there's a slight possibility of escape. I have to make a decision.

"Fine, I'll choose," I say, my voice soft and shaky. "I choose Madison—"

I pause for a moment. I close my eyes. I can't say it.

But then my eyes shoot open. I react with my gut, not knowing what I'm saying. There's a part of me deep down that wants to choose the person I actually want to marry and want to kill. I can't stop myself.

I say, "I choose Jennie to marry and Madison to kill."

All the women in the room are shocked by my words. Even Jennie can't believe I chose her. Bella and Eve look at me like I'm crazy.

"No, I told you I won't marry you!" Jennie says. "Kill me. I'd rather die."

Madison looks around, not believing what she heard. "Wait… You chose me for kill? You want to kill me? You said you wouldn't…"

I look at her face with tears in her eyes. I can't believe I chose her. I didn't want to. The words just came out.

"I'm sorry," I tell her. "I didn't mean it…"

"Then choose her not me!" Madison cries. "She doesn't even want to marry you. Why would you kill me and not her?"

I just tell her I'm sorry over and over again. I'm such

an idiot. I have to take it back. The only choice was to kill Jennie.

"The decision has been made!" Principal Games says. "All you have to do is kill Madison and you get to go home with your new bride, Arlo. Fail to kill her before the time runs out, and none of you will go home ever again."

"No!" Madison cries. "This isn't fair!"

Eve steps forward. "Kill the bitch, Arlo! She needs to die."

"You have to hurry," Bella urges. "Don't think about it. Just do it."

I shake my head. I don't think I can kill her. I should have chosen Jennie. If she was willing to be the one to be killed, then maybe I could have followed through. But looking at Madison's face, so filled with fear and desperation, how can I go through with it?

But my body moves without thinking. I step toward Madison. I have to kill her with my bare hands, but I don't know how to do it. Should I break her neck like the guy in the video? How do you even break someone's neck?

As I move toward her, Madison runs. She races to the other side of the room, tossing desks between us.

"Get away from me!" she cries.

I go after her, but she's faster than me. She runs away. She won't let me anywhere near her.

"We can't let her live," Bella says.

Eve nods in agreement. "Get her!"

Both Bella and Eve charge Madison, cutting her off. Eve tackles her and Bella grabs her arms, pulling them behind her back. The two women hold the crying girl in place as she struggles and frantically begs for mercy. They have no pity for her whatsoever, too focused on saving themselves.

"Do it, Arlo," Bella tells me. "You have to kill her."

"No!" Madison yells. "Kill Jennie, not me!"

I go to her, holding out my trembling hands. I don't know what's gotten over me. I feel like somebody else is controlling my body, like my survival instinct is taking over. My hands wrap around her neck and I begin to squeeze.

"That's it, Arlo!" Principal Games cries with glee. "Kill the bitch! Murder her! Show us that you're a man!"

"Do it!" Eve cries. "End this!"

I squeeze tighter. The look on Madison's face fills me with disgust. There's so much hate and fear in her eyes. I divert my attention, not wanting to see her expression anymore. I don't want that look to haunt me for the rest of my life. Instead, I look at Eve. The bitch seems like she's almost enjoying this.

Eve cries, "Kill her! Kill her! Finish it!"

As I choke Madison, feeling her body writhe and thrash in my grip, I imagine it's Eve's neck my hands are wrapped around. I squeeze it so tight that it feels like it's going to break under my strength. Her body becomes weak and she goes limp in Bella's arms, but I keep choking her. I strangle her until I'm sure that she's dead.

When Eve and Bella let her go, Madison's body falls to the floor. They check for a pulse.

"She's dead," Bella says.

I step back. I can't believe what I've just done. I drop into a chair and put my face on the desk. Then I just start to cry. I don't care who hears me. I sob like it was my own sister that I just murdered. I scream and pound my fist against my knee. I want to kill someone. I want to hurt the people who made me do this.

But the other women in the room don't feel the same as I do. Relief washes over them. Eve falls to the ground and takes a deep breath. Bella leans against the wall next to her, wiping her brow and placing her head against her shoulder.

"Congratulations!" Principal Games says. "You have passed three of the four challenges! Now all that's left is to sign the wedding certificate and you can all go home."

But as he says this, not a person in the room is excited. We all want to go home, but we also know that life after this will never be the same.

The door opens up and Principal Games enters with three of his armed guards. They all wear black hoods covering their faces. Principal Games is a tall skinny man who wears a gray suit with a matching hat on top of his hood. He holds up some paperwork.

He says, "Jennie and Arlo, it's time for you to get married. I'm sorry we couldn't have a more romantic wedding ceremony for you, but this will have to do." He slams the paperwork on a desk and then lays a pen on top of it. "This is a real wedding certificate. It is legally binding and you will now be known as husband and wife the second you sign it."

When we look over at Jennie, Eve and Bella get worried. They wonder if she'll really sign it. If she refuses then all of this will be for nothing. They'll just kill us anyway.

But Jennie doesn't hesitate.

"This means nothing," Jennie tells me. "I'm not really your wife, no matter what this paper says."

She picks up the pen and signs her name. Then she drops it and steps aside. Bella and Eve push me to the desk and put the pen in my hand. They don't leave until I sign it.

When it's all over, Principal Games says, "That concludes it. You all get to live. Well, all of you except for Madison." He turns to me. "Geez, Arlo. You were kind of cold choosing the most innocent girl in the room. No one predicted that. The betting pool was rooting for Eve or Bella to die. No one suspected you'd choose Madison."

I don't respond. I regret it myself. If I had to do it all over again I would have chosen differently. Jennie should have been kiss, Bella should have been fuck, Madison should have been marry, Eve should have been kill. I'm sure that would have been the right choice. As hard of a decision it was to make, it's the only one I would have been comfortable with. But it's too late. The damage has already been done. And now I have to live with it for the rest of my life.

CHAPTER FIVE

We are all chloroformed one by one. Eve first and then Bella. As they do it, I look at Jennie and she glares at me like I'm the biggest scumbag in the world. She hates me for choosing her. Of all the girls I could have chosen for marry, she's the worst one. I have no idea how I could be so stupid. She doesn't stop glaring at me as the rag is put over her mouth and she falls to sleep.

"Great job, Arlo," Principal Games says, once all the women are unconscious. "You played a really interesting game. I think this was one of my favorites. I had no idea you had it in you. Honestly, I assumed you would have wimped out and let us kill you all. But you pulled through." He pats me on the back. "We'll make a man out of you, yet. Take this experience with you as an opportunity to get stronger. Have more confidence. We created this game for guys like you. Cowardly, wimpy guys who take shit from women every day of their lives. But this is a man's world. Don't you forget that. Men take what they want. They don't wait for permission. Make this world your own, Arlo."

He goes to Jennie and lifts up her head by her hair. I move in to stop him, but his guards hold me back.

Principal Games grabs her breast through her shirt. "This shit is all yours now. You can do whatever you want with it. Make her submit to you. Turn her into your bitch." He squeezes her boob tightly. "Show her what a man you are."

I push against the guards. "Don't fucking touch her!"

Principal Games lets her go and holds up his hands. "Yes, sir. I get it. She's your property now. You don't need another man touching her like this." He steps closer to me and nods to Jennie's unconscious body. "Do you want to have a go with her right now? She's asleep. She's not in a place to refuse. If you want, we could leave the room for a while and let you have your way with her while she's unconscious. It wouldn't be a problem for us. As long as you let us film it, we'd love to give you the opportunity."

I look at him with disgust. I can't believe he would even suggest such a thing.

"Consider it a reward for doing so well in the game," Principal Games says. "You deserve it. Be a man. Have fun. In fact, you can fuck any of these women if you want. Use them all. We don't care. We live for this shit."

I shake my head at him and say, "No. No way. I'm not doing that."

Of all the things I've had to do today, that would have been the worst of them. Even though I killed Madison, I at least didn't have a choice in the matter. With this, it would be rape. I won't do it. No matter what they say,

I would never go that far.

"You disappoint me, Arlo," Principal Games says. "Well, you'll have to fuck her eventually. As we mentioned, you'll need to have at least one child together within the next ten years. It's the only way to prove you're really married. There's no point in getting married without having kids, right? Otherwise, you'd be an idiot. No bitch is worth spending the rest of your life with unless she provides you with her offspring. Am I right?"

He looks at me with excitement, but I don't return his enthusiasm. He's an asshole. I would never be a man like him. He's everything I hate about being a man.

"Whatever," says Principal Games. "You'll learn eventually. Every man has to learn their place in the world at some point."

He pours the bottle of chloroform into the rag and says, "And that place is at the top."

Then he shoves the rag in my face. I don't fight it. I breathe in the chemical until I pass out.

When I wake up, I find myself in a studio apartment, lying on a bed next to Jennie. She's still asleep. I decide not to bother her. I get up feeling sick to my stomach. I'm starving and feel like I want to throw up. I'm dizzy. I have no idea how long I was asleep. It could have been days.

I look around the room and find a note on the small dining table near the kitchen area.

It reads:

Congratulations, newlyweds!

This apartment is your new love nest. Both of your names are on the lease and the first three months are paid for. You're welcome, by the way. After that? You'll have to figure out how to pay the rent yourself. We got you the most affordable place in the area near your campus, but feel free to upgrade if you want. Just remember, you have to stay living together. Those are the rules, my friends.

Let me remind you of the deal: stay together for life, sleep in the same bed, and pop out at least one kid within the next ten years. Easy, right? We consider ourselves perfect matchmakers with a 100% success rate. Nobody's ever broken the rules before, so don't be the idiots who ruin our perfect record.

Here's the fun part. You are free to cheat on each other as much as you want and even have an open relationship. We don't care about that stuff. Just don't spend more than two weeks apart from each, and don't fail to produce offspring. You'll figure it out. I have faith in you.

Break the rules? You're either dead or forced to play the game again. Neither of you want that, do you?

Try to be happy. Life is short. Nothing good will come from resenting us for doing this to you. Who knows? Maybe you'll fall in love and live happily ever after. It's happened before. Don't think of this as a punishment. Think of it as an opportunity. I'm rooting for the both of you. Be a good man, Arlo. Be a good woman, Jennie. This world will be better if you just accept your roles, your proper genders, and live your life to its fullest. Good luck to you both! I sincerely mean that.

Your pal,
Principal Games

After I read the note, I crumple it up and throw it away in the kitchen trash can. I can't believe that scumbag. Does he really think we could have a happy life after all that? Fuck him. Fuck all of them. I'll never forgive him for the rest of my life.

When Jennie wakes, she sits up and adjusts the glasses on her face. She groans and gets to her feet. Then she rushes to the bathroom as though she has to puke. She clearly knows I'm here, but she doesn't look at me. As she goes to the bathroom, she leaves the door open. I hear the urine stream echoing through the tiny studio apartment. When she comes back, I'm sitting in a chair at the dining table. She looks at me once and then turns away.

"This is where we're supposed to live," I tell her.

Then I explain what was in the note. I mention that we have the place rent free for a few months and then have to pay rent ourselves. I remind her of the rules and how we have to stay together no matter what. But for some reason, I don't tell her about how we're allowed to have an open relationship. I can't handle the thought of being married to a woman who sleeps with other guys, even if it's not a real marriage. I'll understand if she does it anyway. She has a boyfriend, after all. But I won't offer up the information. I feel like an asshole for it, but I'd rather not let her know.

"I'm sorry," I tell her. "I didn't mean for any of this to happen."

She doesn't look at me with pity or disgust. She just sits on the bed, trying to get over the effects of the anesthetic.

"Save it," she says. "You're an asshole, but it wasn't your fault."

I nod my head. "I know. I just feel bad anyway."

She stares me in the eyes. "Look. We got out of that alive. I appreciate you saving me, I do. But it was the wrong decision. You should have married Madison. At least then you might have had a chance of happiness. But you chose me. I'll never love you. No matter what happens, I promise you that I'll hate you until the day I die."

Then she goes for the door.

"Where are you going?" I ask.

"They said we can be apart for two weeks without punishment, right?" she asks. "I'll see you in two weeks. I'm going to be with my boyfriend."

Then she walks out.

I put my hands on my face. This is going to be a disaster. I have no idea what I'm going to do. She hates me. I'll never be able to marry anyone else. I'm stuck with her. And I know that the only thing left for us is misery.

Weeks pass. I see Jennie only a few times in a month. I move my stuff in from my dorm, telling my roommate that I got married and plan to live with my wife from now on. He freaks out at me, shocked that I was even dating a woman let alone getting married to one. I don't fill him in on the details. I just leave it up to his imagination. It takes longer for Jennie to move her stuff in. She spends most of her time at her old place where she lived with her friends, or her boyfriend's place. But eventually she moves in completely. She can't afford two rents so she gives up her room with her friends so they can get a new roommate.

When we sleep together, Jennie keeps her distance. She sleeps on the far end of the bed, leaving at least a few feet between us. I do the same, out of respect. I wish she would sleep closer. I wish I could feel her warmth next to mine, even if it's just our shoulders touching. But she wants nothing to do with me. I'm just a reminder of the horrible game we were forced to play. She doesn't even talk to me much. It's like she's ghosting me in my own home. It's frustrating. Part of me loves the fact that I'm married to her, if she would only accept me. But I'm just a disgusting asshole who pales in comparison to her perfect boyfriend.

I tell my mother that I got married and she seems surprised yet supportive. She tells me that she thought I was gay and can't believe I actually ended up with a woman. I don't know how to take that, but I just let her know that I'm happy and that everything is okay. I don't tell her about the game. I don't tell her about how my wife really hates me and wants nothing to do with me. I wish I could tell somebody about what I went through, but she's not the person to speak with about this. Nobody is. The only ones who would understand are others who have been in my situation, but I'll never be able to meet anyone like that. For all I know, the other guys in my position loved every second of it. They might have even seen it as the greatest moment of their lives.

My mother agrees to pay my half of the rent instead of paying for my dorm, but urges me to get a job. She wishes me luck, but expresses her disappointment for not having a wedding. She only has one son. She wishes that she would have been able to experience her son getting married. But she isn't able to make me feel guilty. My mother's happiness is the least of my concerns. She tells me that she can't wait to meet Jennie, but I tell her that she's really busy and I don't know when that will be. I know Jennie has no intention to take our marriage seriously. It'll be a very long time before my mother will ever get to meet her, and I'm sure she won't be happy once she does. I'm sure she'll say that I made a bad choice by marrying such a cold and distant woman. I'll try to avoid that moment for as long as I can.

I get a job at Carl's Jr. to have a little extra money and give Jennie as much space as she needs. It's not a very fun job, placing meat patties on a flame-broiling conveyor belt and then assembling burgers to be as messy as possible. The tricky part is wrapping the burgers. I just can't get the hang of it. Every burger I send out, the wrapping is just sloppy and looks bad. The manager gets mad at me almost every day, but I don't get fired. They just have to wrap the burgers themselves if they want them to look nice and pretty. I really don't care either way.

Jennie's boyfriend breaks up with her after a couple of months. Even though she made it seem like they were in love like no other couple in the world, he just couldn't stand the idea of her living with another man. She explained that she didn't love me and that our marriage was not real. She made up the lie that it was an arranged marriage that our parents forced us into, but he didn't buy it. He knew she didn't have any real parents and that the last foster parents she had stopped talking to her once she turned eighteen and left home. He couldn't live with the idea of being the other man. He told her that she had to choose between me and him and she had no choice but to choose me. He didn't take it very well. He said he never wanted to see her ever again.

When Jennie told me about this, she blamed me for everything. She said it was my fault for choosing her for marry. Any other option, she would have been okay with. Even kill. But marrying me was the absolute worst choice. I feel terrible when she tells me this. I beat myself up for days. But then I think about it. Why does it have to be my fault? She could have volunteered for kiss instead of Bella. If she did that it would have been fine for her. Maybe I would have been with Bella or Madison instead of her. Maybe they would have actually talked to me like a normal person. I don't need to be loved. I just don't want to be treated like an absolute creep every single day of my life.

But maybe I deserve it. I'm a murderer, after all. Maybe I don't deserve happiness. Maybe this is my punishment for being such a horrible human being. She has every right to hate me. I don't deserve happiness or respect or peace after everything I've done.

For the next few weeks, I just do my job and attend

my classes, trying to do the best I can with the life I have. I'm miserable. I want to die. But I keep going. I'm not going to let the game beat me. Otherwise, what was the point of surviving? Why did I go through with everything I did? Was it to save Jennie, who had her life ruined by me? Was it to save Bella and Eve, who held down Madison so that I could kill her and save themselves? It's all pointless. I should have just let us all die. The only one who deserved to live was Madison, yet she was the single person who died to save the rest of us.

I am convinced that I'm the worst person in the entire world.

I see Bella on campus one day. She's waiting for me outside of my German class. When I notice her, I assume it is just a coincidence. I just nod my head and move on. But she chases me down.

"Hey, Arlo," she says, cutting in front of me. "I was looking for you."

I turn to her. She notices the absolute misery in my eyes.

"How are you doing?" she asks. "I wanted to see if you were okay."

I walk around her. "What do you care? I'm fine. Leave me alone."

She grabs me by the arm, not letting go. "I need to make sure you're okay. You and Jennie. How is it going?"

I force myself out of her grip. "Miserable." It's too hard to lie to her. I just tell her how it really is. "Every day is a living hell."

"That's a problem," she says. "For all of us. If your relationship doesn't work, the rest of us will be killed. You have to hang in there for our sake."

For some reason, her words annoy me. "Why should I? Jennie hates every second she's with me. It's horrible." I look away. "I feel like such an asshole every day."

Bella nods. "That's what I thought. Jennie has a boyfriend, doesn't she?"

I shake my head. "Not anymore. He dumped her. She blames me for it, obviously. I don't know how long I can take it."

Bella sighs. "You should have just done what I said. Had you killed Eve and married Madison, this wouldn't have happened. Even if you killed Jennie, it would have been fine. You fucked up."

"You think I don't know that?" I take a deep breath. "Besides, I never wanted to kill Eve, either. No one was the right choice."

"Why didn't you just choose who you really wanted? If I was in your shoes I wouldn't have let the men choose for me. I would have gone with the ones that I wanted to choose no matter what they said. Your weakness is going to get us all killed."

I step away from her. I have no idea why she would say this to me. What I did has already been done. I can't take it back. I have to live with my horrible decisions.

"Look," she says. "I don't want to die after all that. I

need to know if you're going to be able to hold it together. Can you do that?"

I have no idea how to answer her. I just say, "I don't know. It's up to Jennie."

"Then we should go to the police and tell them what happened. Maybe they can protect us. I've been talking with Eve and she wants revenge for what they did to us. We have to tell our story. We can't let them get away with this."

I shake my head. "We can't do that. They'll know if we go to the police. Principal Games said his employers are powerful and dangerous. They wouldn't let us talk."

"We don't know if that's true. He could have been lying. If your relationship was fine then I wouldn't bother, but if you are going to break up then I'd rather risk going to the cops."

"Will they even believe us?"

"Well, they surely know Madison has gone missing. They can't ignore that."

"I don't know. I don't think I can."

Bella gets in my face. "Then you better make things right with Jennie. Don't just let her ignore you. Be the nicest guy in the world. Treat her like a queen. Make her fall in love with you. Stop being a miserable little prick and maybe she'll see you as someone worth spending the rest of her life with."

When she says this to me, I don't know how to respond. I wish I could do such a thing. I wish I could just win Jennie over and be the husband that she deserves, maybe even better than her ex-boyfriend. Perhaps Bella is right. Perhaps there is hope for me to win her over. If she could fall in love with me, then everything would be fine. I'd be able to spend the rest of my life with the woman of my dreams and nothing bad will ever happen to us ever again.

"I'll try," I tell Bella. "I'll do what I can."

With that, she is satisfied. She doesn't try to convince me any further and no longer feels the need to go to the police.

"Okay," she tells me. "I'm counting on you. Make your relationship work. If it doesn't then let me know, will you? I'll give you my cell number."

She puts her contact information into my phone.

"Good luck," she says.

Then she walks away, heading back toward her dorm. As she goes, I watch her ass in her tight jeans. It is a perfect shape. Big and soft, but not too fat. Perfectly round in a way that makes it hard to take your eyes off of. I really wish I did choose Bella to marry instead of Jennie. I would have been able to look at that ass all day long. If it was her I think I could be happy. She seems like the kind of woman who would have tried to make it work. She's so confident and strong-willed. She's just like the man I wish I could be.

On the way home, I imagine all the ways I can win Jennie over. Maybe I should bring her flowers every day or make her delicious meals that will show her how much I could love her. But I'm not that good of a cook and flowers might seem like I'm coming on too strong. She might come to hate me even more if I did that, especially so soon after her breakup. I just have to be nice and accommodating. I've tried to do that already, by giving her a lot of space. But by doing it, I haven't been able to spend much time with her. If we don't spend more time together, then she'll never fall for me. Maybe I should quit my job. Maybe I should work different hours. I'm not sure. But I have to do something. If I don't then it's going to be a disaster.

When I get home, I see Jennie packing her things.

"What are you doing?" I ask, going to the bed where all of her belongings are spread out.

She doesn't stop packing, putting her stuff in a suitcase as quickly as she can.

"I'm sorry," she says. "I can't do this."

"What do you mean?"

"I can't be married to you anymore. I don't care what happens to me. I'm getting out of here."

"You can't. If you leave, they're going to kill us."

She doesn't seem to care in the slightest. "I'm going to go into hiding. I'm going far away from here and never coming back. I suggest you do the same."

I'm flooded with panic. "You can't be serious. That's not going to work. They'll find you. We'll all die. Don't you care about the others? Bella and Eve?"

"Fuck those bitches," she says. "I don't care what happens to them. Besides, there's no guarantee they'll kill us if we leave each other. They could have just been bluffing. Why would they put so much effort into keeping us together? Think about it. They probably organized that game as some kind of snuff film to show to rich clients. Nobody cares if we stay married. There's no money in it for them. They'll probably just let us go."

"You don't know that," I tell her.

I find myself pulling her belongings away from her suitcase, forcing her to unpack. She has to stay. There's no way around it. But as I pull at her clothes, I realize that I'm doing it not because I'm worried about our safety. I just don't want her to go. I had plans to make her fall in love with me. That will never happen if she leaves.

Jennie pushes me back. "I'm willing to risk it. Even if they are watching us and plan to kill us, I need to get away from you. I'm sorry. There's no way I'm spending another day in this place."

She grabs what she has in her suitcase and closes it, leaving the rest behind. Then she goes for the door. I don't try to stop her.

Before she leaves, Jennie looks back. In a soft voice, she says, "Thanks for not killing me, even after I asked you to."

Then she goes through the door and leaves me alone in our apartment. I drop to the bed. Even though I don't blame her for going, I wish I could have said something to make her stay. I wish there was something I could have done to make her love me. I know that I'll be alone until the day I die. And if Principal Games was serious about his threat, it won't be very long before that happens.

I don't run away like Jennie did. I stay in the apartment, going on with my life like nothing happened. If I am to be killed, I'm willing to let it happen. I deserve it after all I've done. My only hope is that she was right about the people behind the game. Maybe they really don't waste the resources to keep tabs on us. It makes sense that it was all just an empty threat. I decide I'll just wait and see what happens.

I text Bella and tell her that Jennie left me. I assume that she would want us to get together and go to the police, but she just responds with: I'm sorry to hear that. Then she says: Just hang tight. I'll figure out what to do.

But that's the last I hear from her. Days pass. She doesn't respond to any of my texts. I worry they already got her. Maybe she tried to go to the police and the police handed her over to our captors. Or maybe she ditched her phone so that she could go into hiding. Either way, I don't plan to do anything on my own. I'm just going to continue my life, the little of it I have left, and wait for the inevitable to come.

After a month, nothing happens. I am not shot in the street. I don't hear from Bella or Jennie. I am just free to live my life. I finish the school year. I get promoted to assistant manager at my job. Everything seems to be going fine and it doesn't seem like anything bad is going to happen to me. But still, I'm not able to relax. It could still happen at any time.

I tell my mother that Jennie and I broke up. We're

not officially divorced, but I don't expect to ever see her again. My mother feels bad for me and decides to send me more money. She tells me that I'll find somebody else. I tell her that I love her, just in case I never hear from her again. She doesn't tell me that she loves me back. She is too busy making dinner for my youngest sister and cuts off the call so she can get back to cooking. I really hope that's not the last time I ever hear from her.

It's okay, though. I understand that she's busy. I'm sure she loves me, too. I don't need to hear it to know she does. Even if it was possibly the last opportunity she might have had to do so.

CHAPTER SIX

I wake up in the same classroom I was in during the game. I would recognize it anywhere. The same claustrophobic space full of junior high desks and brick walls instead of windows. At first, I think I must be dreaming. I'm just being haunted by my sins of the past.

But then I hear a familiar voice.

"What the fuck…" she says.

I turn to her. It's Eve. She's lying behind me. She sits up, rubbing her eyes.

This isn't a dream. We're really back here, in the classroom. I don't remember being kidnapped again, but they must have gotten us somehow. They must have brought us back here so that we could play the game again, because Jennie left me.

"Eve?" I ask, going to her. "Are you okay?"

She pushes me away. "Get the fuck off me."

As she gets her senses back, she realizes where we are.

"Oh fuck," she says. "Not again…"

But when I look around the room, expecting to see Bella and Jennie, I realize the others in the room are people I don't know. There are three guys lying on the floor behind a row of desks. They wake up, confused about where they are or what has happened to them.

Based on the looks on their faces, they don't know anything about this place or the game that is going to be played. I go to them and help them to their feet. All three of them are much larger than me. They look like frat boys or football players. Every one of them is far more of a man than I am. They weigh so much I can barely even get them to their feet.

"Where are we?" a bulky Filipino guy with a shaved head asks, trying to shake the drowsiness out of his eyes.

"Oh shit…" Eve says.

I look back at her. There's a smile on her face.

"I'm the chooser this time," she says. "I'm you. I get to be the one to decide."

As she says this, reality dawns on me. There are four guys and one girl. If we are playing the same game, Eve will be the one who gets to decide our fate. It won't be me. Thank God it won't be me. But if Eve is the one who gets to choose, then I'm in very big trouble. In fact, I might be absolutely fucked.

"This is more like it," Eve says, brushing dust from her way-too-short shorts. "I'm okay with this."

A blond frat boy asks, "What happened? Did I party too hard last night? I don't remember anything."

I try to explain, but Eve cuts me off.

"You're going to play a game," she tells him. "We've all been kidnapped and they're going to force us to do some horrible shit. But this time it's going to slay."

She is practically dancing with happiness, not giving a shit about how the others feel.

I explain for her. “We’ve gone through this before. Several months ago, Eve and I were kidnapped and forced to do this. It was the worst thing that ever happened to me.”

A dark-haired guy with a tall nose and a pronounced forehead comes forward. “Bro, you’re not making sense. My head is pounding. Just tell me where the bathroom is.”

He goes to the door and tries the handle, but it doesn’t budge.

“What the fuck? We’re locked in.”

He kicks on the door. It doesn’t budge.

“They won’t let us go until we play the game,” Eve says.

“What game?” the blond guy asks.

He stands next to me. This close, I realize how tall he is. He’s probably six four, maybe six five. Not quite as muscular as the others, but probably the most handsome. He could be a male model. I feel inadequate being in his presence. It’s like being in a room with a movie star.

“The game is called Kiss, Fuck, Marry, Kill,” I tell him.

Eve nods excitedly. “Yep. I get to choose one of you to kiss, which one to fuck, which one to marry, and which one to kill.” She looks over at me with a disgusted face. “He got to choose last time and I had to fuck him. It was horrible. He’s got the grossest dick I’ve ever seen.”

The guys just laugh, but they don’t seem to understand the situation they’re in. They seem like they’re ready to start a keg party and this is just a fun thing to do to pass the time.

I explain to them how the game works, but they don't seem to believe me. Even when Eve backs me up, they just think this is some kind of joke. That is, until Principal Games comes on the intercom system.

"Attention students!"

Principal Games' voice sends a chill down my spine. I never thought I'd ever have to hear him for the rest of my life. Even if I were killed after Jennie left me, I never thought I'd come here again.

"Welcome to round two of Kiss, Fuck, Marry, Kill," Principal Games continues. "We have three new contestants and two familiar faces. I would call Arlo a reigning champion, but he was a disappointment to us. He couldn't man up and keep his house in order, so now he's back to go through it all over again. Only now he's at the mercy of the woman who hates him more than any of the other survivors."

Eve looks over at me, revulsion in her eyes. "You know I had to get an abortion because of you, right? Your fucking diseased spunk ended up getting me pregnant. Thank God I caught it in time. There was no way I was going to keep that thing."

When she says this, my jaw drops. I knew we were forced to have unprotected sex, but I had no idea that just one time would result in a pregnancy. The news sends a chill through my spine. I can't believe that happened to her.

"I'm sorry," I say. "Had I known I—"

She cuts me off. "You would have what? Helped me raise it? Help pay for the abortion? Just fuck off, Arlo. I didn't want your help."

Principal Games chuckles. Then he continues, "So it seems you all know the rules. Eve here gets to choose which one she gets to kiss, which one she gets to fuck, which one she gets to marry, and which one she gets to kill. Prepare yourselves, boys. We don't normally have a woman in the position of power. But this is a special occasion. We couldn't pass this opportunity by."

He continues explaining the rest of the rules to the newcomers. He tells them about what happens if you get married. He explains how we'll all die if Eve doesn't make a decision. He even shows the video of the past contestants. The last video is one I recognize instantly. It's a video of us. Me, Bella, and Eve. It shows me killing Madison. Seeing it again, from the camera's perspective, fills me with disgust. I can't look at it. I seem like such a monster as I murder the girl to save myself.

The other men glare at me with disgust as I choke the life out of the poor girl. Even though Eve was there, too, holding down the girl as I choked her, they only blame me for the act. Maybe they just don't want to get on Eve's bad side, or maybe they are the type to think women are always guiltless, but the room becomes tense. All of their frustration and anger for being put in this situation is directed at me.

"That was pretty cold, bro," the dark-haired guy says.

The guy with the shaved head says, "Yeah, what the fuck is wrong with you?"

"I didn't have a choice!" I explain. "They would have killed all of us if I didn't do it."

But they don't seem to empathize with my position. They just keep their distance, seeing me as the worst human being in the world. It's like they think I enjoyed doing it, that I wanted to be in the place to kill a woman. And there's nothing I can say to make them think otherwise.

The game starts immediately. Eve has two hours to make her first choice, but she doesn't need that much time. She stands before us, eating up every second of this. It's like she's been waiting for this for months. She finally gets to have some payback for what she had to go through. And the four of us will have to endure her revenge.

"So which one should I choose?" she asks, walking in front of us with a smile on her face, looking us up and down one at a time.

I get impatient. I know she's going to choose me for kill, so I just want to get it over with as soon as possible.

"Just tell us who you want to kiss, Eve," I say. "Pick any of them. It doesn't matter."

Eve looks at me and moans. "I'm not choosing kiss first. Fuck that. I'll save that for last. The most important choice is marry. I don't want to spend my life with some loser. The others don't matter as much."

She backs up and claps her hands together. Then she says, "Okay, tell me what you all do for a living."

The blond guy shrugs. "I'm just a student. I don't have a job."

The guy with the shaved head says, "I work at the snowboard shop on the weekends."

Eve gets annoyed at their answers. "Then tell me what your parents do. Who comes from the richest family? If I have to get married, the guy better have some money."

"My parents have money," the dark-haired guy says.

"Mine too," the other guys say.

I don't respond. I know Eve doesn't want to marry me anyway, even if I did come from a rich family.

"Well, that's promising," Eve asks. "How much are your family's homes worth?"

Two of them say their homes are worth over five million dollars. Eve's eyes light up after she hears this.

"Seriously?" Then she nods her head. "Not bad. What are your majors?"

"I'm studying medicine," says the guy with the shaved head. "My parents want me to be a doctor."

"I'm going for an entrepreneur degree," the dark-haired guy says. "I plan to start my own computer business. My father is ready to put up the money for it. It's going to be huge."

"A CEO, huh?" she asks, excitement in her eyes. "Okay, I'll choose you. Doctors are okay, but I'd rather be with a guy who owns his own company. That will give me the life I want."

She pushes the dark-haired guy aside. "Wait over there until the game is over. You're safe."

The dark-haired guy seems confused. "Is this real? I'm actually supposed to marry you?"

"Don't worry about it," Eve says, not able to stop

smiling. "I'll talk to you later."

The dark-haired guy does as he's told.

I realize that we've never introduced ourselves. I don't know the names of any of these guys. Neither does Eve. I can't believe she would just choose a guy to marry without even knowing his name first. But she seems to be having a good time. She really doesn't care about the men in the room. She's just drunk on the power of being in the position to decide all of our fates. She probably doesn't see a single one of us as human beings anymore.

"Next, I'll choose fuck," Eve says, she steps to the guys, measuring them up. "Drop your pants. All of you."

The men just stand there, not sure if she's serious. Eve gets annoyed.

"Come on," she says, clapping her hands together. "Chop chop. I want to see which one of you has the biggest junk. Whoever has the best dick gets to fuck me."

The guys look at each other, feeling a bit awkward and unsure if they should really follow her directions. But after a brief pause, they all comply. They unzip their pants and pull them down. Before I can get mine off, Eve stops me.

"Not you, Arlo," she tells me. "I already know what you're packing and I don't need to see it again. Put it away. I'm definitely not choosing you."

As the other two guys stand there with their dicks

out, Eve goes to them, examining their merchandise. She leans down to the guy with the shaved head and takes a good look at his penis. "Not bad. I like it."

Then she goes to the blond and her jaw drops open. "Holy shit. What the hell is this?"

When I look over, I noticed that the blond guy is incredibly well-endowed. Not only does he have the looks and physique of a model, he's also got a dick that most guys would kill for.

"I'm definitely choosing you," she says, grabbing the blond guy by the shoulders and pulling him forward. "You look like you know what to do with that thing."

The guy is confused. "So I'm just supposed to fuck you? Right here and now?"

She shakes her head. "Not yet. Go wait with the other one. I'll get to you later."

He just pulls his pants up and goes to stand with the dark-haired guy. It's just me and the bald guy left. I glance over at him. He doesn't seem to be too concerned with what is about to come next. Maybe he knows that I'm the one Eve will choose to kill, or maybe the reality of the situation hasn't kicked in yet. Either way, I'm the only one in the room who's shitting his pants right now.

"Great job, Eve!" Principal Games says over the intercom. "This is the fastest game of Kiss, Fuck, Marry, Kill that's ever been played! We've never had a contestant like you before. You know what you want and don't hesitate for a second. Arlo, this is how you should have been. This chick is proving to be more of a man than you'll ever be."

But his words of encouragement don't win Eve over. She turns to the camera and says, "Shut the fuck up, asshole! You're ruining the moment for me. Just let me do my thing."

Principal Games chuckles. "Very well, missy. Have it your way. It's the final round, let's see how you do."

Eve comes up to me and the other guy. She looks both of us in the eyes, glaring deep into our souls.

"So which one of you should I kiss and which one should I kill?" she asks. "The best and the worst option. Oh, isn't this hard?" She looks at me. "Is this how it felt for you, Arlo? Was it exciting knowing you had the lives of four women in your hands?"

I shake my head. "It was horrible."

"Yeah, right," she says.

"I didn't choose any of them. I let all of you make the choices for me."

Eve rolls her eyes. "Tell that to Madison. She didn't choose to die."

I look away. "I just wanted to save Jennie."

"And how did that work out for you? She left you, didn't she? Bella told me all about it." She gets closer, talking right in my face. "You're the reason we're back here, aren't you? You didn't follow the rules, and so they brought us back to play the game again. They're going to go after Bella and Jennie next, if they haven't already. Because of you, we have to do this all over again. It's your fault. All of this is your fault. I'm so going to choose you as kill."

When she says that, I begin to panic. My whole body trembles with fear. I knew she would choose me for kill, but I didn't want to believe it. Knowing that she really is going to do it, that it's really going to happen, fills me with terror. I don't want to die. Even though I have nothing to live for, even though I thought I would be okay if a woman were given the decision to kill me, I still want to live.

"Don't kill me," I tell her, tears running down my face. "Please. It wasn't my fault. I never wanted anything bad to happen to any of you."

Eve just smirks at me in response. She doesn't say another word.

She goes to the other guy and leans in. "Come here, cutie. Give me a kiss."

Then she wraps her arms around him and kisses him like she means it. But the guy just stands there, not sure what to do. He lets her stick her tongue in her mouth, but he just looks in my direction with an awkward expression on his face. He doesn't seem to know what's going on.

Eve pulls away and sighs with satisfaction. "Awww. That was nice." She looks at the others. "Aren't we having fun, boys? It's not so bad, is it?"

The blond guy looks at her with a dumb expression. "So are you going to fuck me now?"

She waves him away. "Not yet. I want to get the messy business over with first." She looks at me. "Arlo. I'm going to kill you now. Are you okay with that?"

I shake my head. "Please…"

She puts her hands around my neck.

She smiles. "Are you ready?"

I just stare into her glistening eyes, unable to speak.

She squeezes gently, applying just a little pressure. Then stops and tilts her head to the side. "Hmmm… This isn't going to work, is it?"

She goes to the camera and waves to get the attention of the people on the other side.

"Mr. Principal?" she asks the camera. "Is it okay if I get a weapon of some kind? I don't think I'm able to kill him with my bare hands. It's not against the rules, is it?"

She looks back at me and winks. It's like she's telling me to be patient and that she'll be right with me in a moment. It would almost be cute if she weren't planning to murder me.

"Very well, Eve," says Principal Games. "Although we don't allow weapons for our male contestants, we understand, as the weaker sex, women are incapable of overpowering a man. Even one as weak as Arlo. We've already prepared a weapon for you. Look under the desk in the back of the room. Third from the left."

Eve perks up and smiles back at the men. She waves at her future husband and goes toward the desk as instructed. The thought comes to me that I should run after her and beat her to the weapon. If I could get to it first, maybe I could prevent her from killing me. But before I take a step, I realize that it would be useless. Even if I got it from her, there's nothing I could do with it. If Eve doesn't kill me, then all of us will die. It's not going to save my life.

Eve goes to the desk and pulls out a gun that was taped underneath. She holds it up and leans it against her shoulder.

"This will do," she says, stepping toward me.

She comes close and drops the barrel of the gun to my chest. Then she looks me in the eye. Even though she has a gun pointed at me, even though she is getting ready to kill me, I can't stop thinking about how pretty she is. The look in her eyes is so calm and filled with confidence. I'm falling in love with her on the spot. Even though making love with her was such a horrible experience, I can't help to think of what it would be like to be with her for real. If only I were more attractive. If only I were more confident and had even an ounce of charisma. Maybe I could have a girl as beautiful as her. Even if she's a total bitch, she's still a woman worth dying for.

She smiles at me, poking the gun in my chest, right where my heart is. The pounding of my heartbeat vibrates through the metal right to her fingers.

"You don't want me to kill you, do you, Arlo?" she asks, a faux-empathetic expression on her face.

"No…" I tell her.

"Come on," she says. "Don't you want to die to save me? That's what you said you'd do in the last game. You said you'd volunteer to die if it meant saving me and the other girls. Did you mean that?"

I nod my head. I know it will mean my death, but I'm not going to lie. If I were given that option, I would have done it in a heartbeat.

Eve pulls the gun away. "Aww… You're so sweet. A horrible fuck, but you're kind of nice in your creepy little way." She takes a step back and points her gun at me again. "Okay, then. If you're willing to die for me, then I'll gladly kill you. You can close your eyes if you want."

I shake my head. If she's going to kill me, I want her to do it while she's looking at me with her beautiful eyes. I want it to be the last thing I see before I go.

Eve holds the gun, her finger on the trigger. The guy standing next to me backs away. The two standing to the side are on the edge of their feet, shocked this is really happening in front of them.

"Boom!" Eve yells, pretending to shoot the gun.

Then she lowers it and laughs her ass off.

"Quit toying with him, Eve," Principal Games says. "Get the job done."

She backs away and leans against one of the desks. "Fuck you, Mr. Principal. I'm not doing a thing you say."

"What does that mean, Eve?" the Principal asks. He has an annoyed tone to his voice.

She laughs again. "It means fuck you! I'm not playing your stupid game."

Her words confuse even me. I step forward. "Eve, what are you doing? You have to kill me."

She shakes her head, a giddy look on her face. "I'm not killing anyone, Arlo. I just wanted to see that stupid look on your face. I actually had you going, didn't I?"

I'm even more confused. "You mean you're just going to refuse to play?"

She sighs, resting the gun against her bare thigh. "I've played enough of this game. But I'm bored now. I don't want to play anymore."

"You can't do that," I tell her. "If you don't do it, all of us are going to die."

She shrugs. "Probably. But I don't want to give the asshole upstairs the satisfaction."

"Are you serious?"

She nods and turns to the other guys in the room. "You boys don't mind if you die, do you? You probably don't have anything good to live for anyway, am I right? From my experience, guys like you are all kind of useless."

They don't look happy with her decision.

"Wait, they'll really kill us?" the dark-haired guy asks.

"I thought you were going to fuck me," the blond guy says.

"Sorry, bro," she says. "I'm not really in the mood."

Her words unnerve the other men, but it's Principal Games who seems to be the most upset.

"What are you doing, Eve?" he asks her. "You have to play the game. If you don't then you will be killed. This isn't a joke."

She shrugs. "Go ahead and kill us then. I told you before, if anything happens to me then you're all going to die. My father will come after you and make you wish you were never born. If you know what's good for you I strongly suggest you just let us go."

"I told you before, Eve," Principal Games says. "Your father doesn't frighten us. We hold all the cards here. Either play the game or die."

She just laughs at him. "This is your last warning." Her voice gets deep and serious. "Let us go or you're fucked."

"Fine," says Principal Games. "Have it your way. Is this your final answer? Do you refuse to play?"

She just flips him off. "I've decided. Go fuck yourself, asshole."

"Very well."

The principal turns off the mic and then gas begins to fill the room.

"What the fuck?" the blond guy yells, stepping away from the wall as gas enters the room behind him.

Eve just smiles, waving the gun around.

"Happy now, Arlo?" she asks me as I cover my mouth and try to hold my breath. "I didn't kill you. If you die, it won't be by my hand."

The guy next to me falls to the ground, face first. Then the other two guys fall. The last thing I see is Eve taking a deep breath and then dropping to the ground as though she's diving into the deep end of a swimming pool.

CHAPTER SEVEN

I wake up surrounded by dead bodies. They aren't the other contestants. They are the men with masks covering their faces who work with Principal Games, the ones who were supposed to kill us. The other three men who were kidnapped with us are still in the spots where they fell. They are in deep sleep, not moving, but they appear to be alive. I pull myself to my feet, trying to stand. Looking around the room, Eve is nowhere to be seen. The door is wide open. Gunshots ring out through the building.

"Eve?" I call out.

I have no idea what happened. Did the knockout gas somehow not affect Eve? Did she kill all of these men?

I step out into the hallway only to see more dead bodies. Someone is running toward me. Before I can get a chance to defend myself, the person grabs me and helps me upright.

When I raise my eyes, I see Bella. She's looking at me with a worried face, asking me if I'm okay.

"Bella?" I ask. "What are you doing here?"

"We put a tracker on Eve," she says. "We figured

they would try to kidnap you again."

I can't believe what she's saying. "What? How?"

Then I look up and see a group of men walking down the hallway, wearing black suits. Eve is with them, hanging on to the man leading the way. He's a large guy. Old, but tough as nails. He has a chiseled face with a gray beard and sunglasses covering his eyes. I can see the resemblance. He must be Eve's father. The one she kept bringing up.

They walk right past me and step into the classroom. Behind me, one of her father's henchmen is dragging a skinny man like a doll. Based on the gray outfit, I can tell that it's Principal Games. He cries and struggles, telling them to take their hands off of him.

"Do you know what the fuck you're doing?" Principal Games cries. "Do you know how much trouble you're all in?"

The henchman dragging him just kicks the principal in the stomach to shut him up.

"Come on," Bella says to me. "Let's see what happens."

We all go into the classroom. The three frat boys are waking up, confused about what happened to them. The henchmen lead them out of the room to escort them out of the facility. Bella and I take our seats as Principal Games is placed at the front of the classroom. I'm surprised by the man's age. I was sure that he would be younger, but he's actually middle-aged, probably in his forties. He just has the mannerisms of someone half his age.

"What is this?" I ask Bella. "Why are we here?"

She looks me deep in the eyes. "Revenge."

Bella tells me the whole story. Unlike the rest of us, Eve didn't hide what had happened to her from her family. She told her father the second she got home. Every gory detail, even what she did with me. Her father was furious. The two of them weren't going to let the assholes get away with it. Her father had been doing what he could to track them down, but wasn't getting anywhere. Not until she learned that Jennie left me. Bella told them everything and knew there wasn't much time before they came after us. That was how Eve's father was able to get them.

I don't know if he just had confidence in his abilities or if he's a complete asshole, but he let his own daughter be the bait. They knew that they wouldn't just kill us. They knew that Principal Games would come after us again, to make us play another game. They didn't get anything out of killing us, just like Jennie predicted. If they wanted us dead, they would force us to play the game again. Eve's father taught her how to hold her breath for long enough to stay conscious when the gas flooded the room. She practiced for weeks. They even predicted they'd give Eve a gun to kill me, allowing her to be armed when they thought the gas knocked us all out. He trained her how to use it. Bella explains that all of the dead bodies in the room were Eve's doing. She murdered them all by herself. I find it hard to believe, but I can't think of any other way she got out of the room alive.

"Are you serious?" I ask Bella, after she tells me the story.

Bella nods. "Yeah, that chick and her dad are absolute psychos."

"But why didn't she kill me?" I ask. "She wants to get her revenge. I was just as horrible to her as any of them."

Bella laughs. "Oh, she got her revenge on you. Did she torture you as much as she said she was going to? She must have been happy that you were kidnapped to be in the game with her. It couldn't have worked out more perfectly for her."

I can't believe it's possible for them to plan all of this. How did they know Eve would have been the one to do the choosing? How would they know she would actually get a gun? It seems too far-fetched to believe. But Bella tells me that Eve's father is just as sick as the men who kidnapped us. He knows the way these people think. He knows exactly what they were going to do even before they know themselves.

Eve hovers over Principal Games, laughing at his situation. She spits in his face and kicks him in the leg.

"You're going to pay for this, bitch," Principal Games says. "I promise that you will. The second my employers find you, it's over. All of you are dead."

Eve's father opens his cell phone and scrolls through it for a moment. Then he hands the phone to the principal. "You mean these employers?"

The look on Principal Games' face goes blank. I can

only imagine that what he's seeing are their dead bodies.

"They were easy enough to find," he tells him. "The only one that I had difficulty tracking down was you. The scumbag who was responsible for kidnapping my daughter. The one I really wanted to punish for this."

Principal Games just kicks his feet like a toddler in frustration. He must know he's fucked. His life is over. There's nothing he can do to save himself now.

"Fine, you win, assholes," he yells. "Fucking kill me. Get it over with."

Eve smiles. She squats down to him. "Oh, but we don't want to kill you. We wouldn't have done all this if all we wanted was for you to die."

A look of horror crosses his face. "What are you going to do to me?"

"We're going to make you play a game," she says.

He looks at her with a perplexed face.

"You like games, don't you Warren?"

"How do you know my name?"

"We know everything about you, Mr. Lynch," Eve's father says. "While we couldn't find you, we were able to get your identity from your employers. We know everything about you. Where you live. Where you work. Who knew that you would end up being a cop?"

"Fuck you, assholes!" he cries. "So fucking what if you know who I am. Just kill me already."

Eve stands up. "Aww… Don't be like that, Warren. Didn't you hear me? We want to play a game with you. We can't kill you until you play with us."

"What game?"

"What else? We're going to play Kiss, Fuck, Marry, Kill."

He looks more confused than scared by this. I have no idea how they plan to make him play it by himself.

He asks, "With who?"

"Aren't you excited to know?" Eve asks, a big smile on her face. "Bring in the other contestants."

After she says this, her father turns to the hallway. "Bring them in."

A group of his henchmen enters, dragging behind four people. A woman and three children. Two girls and one boy. They are gagged and blindfolded, crying and trembling with fear. When Principal Games sees them, his eyes go wide, his lips quiver.

"We didn't just find out who you are, Warren," Eve says. "We also found out who your family is. Your wife and kids. Those are the people you're playing the game with."

The henchman drags his family before him and forces them to the floor. I tense up when I see it. I can't believe this is happening.

"Are they serious?" I ask Bella. "They're not really going to do this, are they?"

Bella just shushes me, but she doesn't seem to know herself. This has to be a joke. They have to just be trying to torture him.

When they take the blindfolds off of his family's eyes, Principal Games freaks out. He screams and kicks his legs as one of the henchmen holds him down.

"You motherfuckers!" he yells. "Let them go. They have nothing to do with this. They're just kids."

"All of the people you abducted were also someone's kids," Eve's father says. "What makes yours special?"

"Go ahead and tell them what you've been doing in your free time," Eve tells him. "Tell them what you would make people do for your sick clients. Tell them who you really are."

Principal Games just cries, shaking his head. He can't admit it to them. His wife tries to speak, but she can't say a word with the gag in her mouth. But from what I can gather, she seems to understand everything. He's probably a husband she knows would be capable of such a thing.

"So now you have to decide," Eve says. "Which one of your family members will you kiss, which one will you fuck, which one will you marry, and which one will you kill?"

"What?" he cries. "You can't make me do that."

"If you don't play, then you all will die," Eve says. "We'll kill your family right in front of you before we finally end your miserable life. So choose. You have two minutes to make your first choice."

"You crazy bitch!" he yells at her. "I'll fucking kill you!"

Eve cocks her head to one side. "Oh, right. You're already married. I guess you have to choose your wife for marry. That leaves your kids. Which one are you going to kiss? Which one are you going to kill?" She leans closer. "And which one are you going to fuck?"

She leans back and laughs her ass off. The tone of her voice is far more deranged than Principal Games' ever was.

"They're really doing this, aren't they?" I ask Bella.

Bella shakes her head. "Eve's a real psychopath. She wouldn't have gone through all this if she didn't mean it."

"I can't do that!" Principal Games cries. "I can't kill one of my children. I can't fuck them."

"Well, then you all just have to die," Eve says.

She puts a gun to his son's head.

"Now, are you going to play, or do I have to pull the trigger?"

Principal Games cracks. He goes from anger and viciousness to a sobbing baby. Tears run down his face. He bows forward, pleading for compassion.

"Please," he says. "I'm begging you. Don't make me do this."

"Did you care that Madison begged for her life before you made us kill her?"

"I'm sorry," he says, his voice full of desperation. "I'm so sorry. I didn't want to do it. I didn't have a choice. It's not my fault."

"You seemed like you were having quite a good time hosting the game show when we were contestants."

"I wasn't. I swear. I hated every second of it. Just please. Kill me. I'll take responsibility. I'll do whatever you want. But don't hurt them. They had nothing to do with this. They're innocent."

Eve gives him a vicious glare. "Everyone you killed was innocent. Everyone who was fucked was innocent. You don't have the right to tell me your family gets to get a free pass."

Then she pulls the trigger. The gunshot echoes through

the room. I don't see it happen. There are too many people blocking my view. But I see the child's body fall to the floor. I hear Principal Games and his family wailing and screaming in shock. The other children cry as loudly as they can with the gags in their mouths.

"Eve… what the fuck?" her father says. "You weren't supposed to do that."

Eve looks at him with an innocent face. "I'm sorry, Daddy… I just got carried away."

"You just killed a kid."

"I know, but I just got caught up in the moment."

Her father takes the gun away from her. But Eve doesn't back away from the game. She recomposes herself.

"Sorry, Warren," she tells the crying father. "I guess you can't choose kill for your son because he's already dead," Eve says. "But consider yourself lucky. If you choose him for fuck then you don't have to scar one of your children for life. But you still have to kill one of them. I want to see you strangle one of your daughters with your bare hands like you forced us to do with Madison."

I can't take it anymore. I stand up and yell, "Eve! That's enough. Don't do this."

She looks back at me with a smile. "Arlo, please don't interrupt. We're just getting good to the good part."

When she turns away from me, I realize there's nothing I can do. With all of the armed men in the room, there's no stopping Eve or her crazy father.

"I need to get out of here," I tell Bella. "I can't watch this."

Bella nods. "Me neither. I'm done."

Nobody pays attention as we leave the room. I squeeze through the armed men in the doorway and escape into the hall. I look back at Principal Games one last time. He's hunched over, completely broken, not able to take his eyes off his dead son's body. He knows that he caused all this. He knows that it's all his fault that he kidnapped the wrong girl, and his whole world came crashing down on him. His family doesn't deserve this, but he brought it on himself.

Bella and I walk as far as we can down the hallway, but we don't leave the building. There are more men at the top of the stairs, keeping a lookout. They probably won't let us leave even if we wanted to.

"What the fuck is wrong with her?" I ask. "She just killed that kid like it was nothing."

Bella just nods. "Yeah, she's a little more fucked up than I thought she was."

I shake my head in disbelief. "If she's that much of a psycho, why did she let me live? I still don't believe she wouldn't kill me after all of that. She had the perfect opportunity. Nobody ever would have known."

"She wouldn't have done that," Bella says. "Eve might be crazy, but she isn't as big of a bitch as you think she is. She's actually pretty cool when you get to know her. Well, at least I thought she was until she killed the kid. Either way, she knows it wasn't your fault. Even if she hated what happened, be thankful she's taking it out on Principal Games instead of you."

"I guess..." I say.

"Besides, why would she kill the father of her child?"

When she says this, I look at her with a puzzled expression. "Excuse me?"

"Didn't she tell you?" Bella asks. "Eve's pregnant. With your child."

"She said she had an abortion."

Bella laughs. "She wanted to but her father wouldn't let her." Then she puts her arm around my shoulder. "Congratulations, bud. You're going to be a daddy!"

Her words send a chill through my spine. I pray that she's just fucking with me. But the look on her face tells me that she's not even slightly joking.

As I slide down the wall, covering my face with my hands, the sound of gunshots rings through the hallway. Dozens of them. Principal Games must not have been able to make a decision, and the armed men opened fire. They shoot so many times that I have to cover my ears so I don't have to hear it. And then all that's left is the sound of Principal Games crying so loudly that it drowns out every other sound in the building.

Then one more gunshot and it's all over.

When they come out of the room, Eve has a big, stupid smile on her face, like she couldn't be more proud of herself for what she's done. She waves at us like we're all old friends and she can't wait to see us and tell us how it all went down.

"That was intense," she tells us. "You should have stayed for it."

We just shake our heads, not interested in the slightest in having seen what was done to those poor children.

The henchmen lead us out of the facility and into the sunlight. We're in the middle of a vast desert, who knows how far away from town. They load Bella and Eve into one of the cars, but before I join them, I am held back by a large man with a gun pointed in my back. He nods for me to move.

The car with Eve and Bella drives off, leaving me in a cloud of dust.

It seems I'm not allowed to leave just yet. The grandfather of my child wants to have a word with me.

BONUS SECTION

This is the part of the book where we would have published an afterword by the author but he insisted on drawing a comic strip instead for reasons we don't quite understand.

Thanks for reading my newest book, *Kiss Fuck Marry Kill.* I hope you enjoyed it!

It's me CM3!

No, it doesn't. A hack is a writer who is skilled enough to make a living from their writing.

Even if their work lacks artistic merit, they are still competent and respected professionals in the field of storytelling.

About 99% of writers will never be able to make a living off of their work, but hacks *do* make a living from their work, which puts them in the top 1% of all writers in the world.

By calling me a hack, you're claiming that I am one of the top writers alive today.

So, thank you very much for that.

Well, artistic merit is different from one person to another. I think my work does have artistic merit, but it's fine if you don't agree.
Besides, people with talent and no skill are a dime a dozen. I'd rather have skill and no talent if I had to choose between the two. Writers who understand even the basics of the craft of writing are incredibly rare these days.

When I went to Clarion West, one of the instructors taught us that you should focus on being a hack when you first start writing.
You want to learn how to build an engine that moves the train. You can fill the train with gold or you can fill it with shit, but as long as the train moves then your audience will ride it all the way to the end.

I'd rather have a stationary train filled with gold than a mobile one filled with shit.

Other writers tend to be more forgiving of stationary trains if they're filled with gold, but the average reader typically won't stand for it. Besides, writers who refuse to learn how to create a good engine tend to fill their trains with gold-painted shit that fools only those looking at surface-level prose.

I'm the kind of writer who fills his train with shit-painted gold. Where the work looks like shit, smells like shit, but is deceptively god tier.

I can guarantee that your work is just shit-painted shit.
Does not think CM3 is god tier

No, there's a little gold in there. You just have to look hard enough.

Buy like twenty of my books and you'll find it eventually.

I hope somebody punches that stupid smug smile off of your face some day.

I get that a lot.
THE END

ABOUT THE AUTHOR

Carlton Mellick III is the Wonderland Book Award-winning author of over 65 novels, including *Quicksand House*, *Bio Melt*, *Cuddly Holocaust* and *Warrior Wolf Women of the Wasteland*, among others. In 2013, he was named one of the top 20 science-fiction writers under the age of 40 by *The Guardian*.

His work has appeared in *The Year's Best Fantasy and Horror*, *The Best Bizarro Fiction of the Decade*, and *Vice Magazine*, and has been translated into Italian, German, Russian, Spanish, Polish, Czech, Turkish, French and Japanese.

He lives in Portland, Oregon, where he obsesses over comic books, micro-brews, video games, and K-pop dance routines.

Visit him online at **carltonmellick.com**

ALSO FROM CARLTON MELLICK III AND
ERASERHEAD PRESS
www.eraserheadpress.com

QUICKSAND HOUSE

Tick and Polly have never met their parents before. They live in the same house with them, they dream about them every night, they share the same flesh and blood, yet for some reason their parents have never found the time to visit them even once since they were born. Living in a dark corner of their parents' vast crumbling mansion, the children long for the day when they will finally be held in their mother's loving arms for the first time... But that day seems to never come. They worry their parents have long since forgotten about them.

When the machines that provide them with food and water stop functioning, the children are forced to venture out of the nursery to find their parents on their own. But the rest of the house is much larger and stranger than they ever could have imagined. The maze-like hallways are dark and seem to go on forever, deranged creatures lurk in every shadow, and the bodies of long-dead children litter the abandoned storerooms. Every minute out of the nursery is a constant battle for survival. And the deeper into the house they go, the more they must unravel the mysteries surrounding their past and the world they've grown up in, if they ever hope to meet the parents they've always longed to see.

Like a survival horror rendition of *Flowers in the Attic*, Carlton Mellick III's *Quicksand House* is his most gripping and sincere work to date.

HUNGRY BUG

In a world where magic exists, spell-casting has become a serious addiction. It ruins lives, tears families apart, and eats away at the fabric of society. Those who cast too much are taken from our world, never to be heard from again. They are sent to a realm known as Hell's Bottom—a sorcerer ghetto where everyday life is a harsh struggle for survival. Porcelain dolls crawl through the alleys like rats, arcane scientists abduct people from the streets to use in their ungodly experiments, and everyone lives in fear of the aristocratic race of spider people who prey on citizens like vampires.

Told in a series of interconnected stories reminiscent of Frank Miller's *Sin City* and David Lapham's *Stray Bullets*, Carlton Mellick III's *Hungry Bug* is an urban fairy tale that focuses on the real life problems that arise within a fantastic world of magic.

STACKING DOLL

Benjamin never thought he'd ever fall in love with anyone, let alone a Matryoshkan, but from the moment he met Ynaria he knew she was the only one for him. Although relationships between humans and Matryoshkans are practically unheard of, the two are determined to get married despite objections from their friends and family. After meeting Ynaria's strict conservative parents, it becomes clear to Benjamin that the only way they will approve of their union is if they undergo The Trial—a matryoshkan wedding tradition where couples lock themselves in a house for several days in order to introduce each other to all of the people living inside of them.

SNUGGLE CLUB

After the death of his wife, Ray Parker decides to get involved with the local "cuddle party" community in order to once again feel the closeness of another human being. Although he's sure it will be a strange and awkward experience, he's determined to give anything a try if it will help him overcome his crippling loneliness. But he has no idea just how unsettling of an experience it will be until it's far too late to escape.

MOUSE TRAP

It's the last school trip young Emily will ever get to go on. Not because it's the end of the school year, but because the world is coming to an end. Teachers, parents, and other students have been slowly dying off over the past several months, killed in mysterious traps that have been appearing across the countryside. Nobody knows where the traps come from or who put them there, but they seem to be designed to exterminate the entirety of the human race.

Emily thought it was going to be an ordinary trip to the local amusement park, but what was supposed to be a normal afternoon of bumper cars and roller coasters has turned into a fight for survival after their teacher is horrifically killed in front of them, leaving the small children to fend for themselves in a life or death game of mouse and mouse trap.

WHY I MARRIED A CLOWN GIRL FROM THE DIMENSION OF DEATH

Timothy is terrified of clowns. He's always found them disturbing and creepy and weird. But now that our world is besieged by clown-like invaders from another dimension, his phobia is spiraling out of control. Timothy has no idea how to handle living in a world full of these cartoonish creatures until he meets a clown girl named Puppy Caterpillars who happens to be the cutest, sweetest girl he's ever encountered. They fall in love and Timothy believes his phobia has finally been cured. But after they get married, Timothy discovers his phobia might have been the only thing keeping him alive.

GLASS CHILDREN

The children of the glass generation are the most sensitive, fragile, entitled, spoiled, lazy, selfish little brats that human society has ever produced. Part of this is due to overprotective parenting, but it is mostly due to the fact that these children are literally made out of glass. Nobody knows why, but one day the human species went through a surreal mutation where babies started being born with delicate hollow glass bodies with no flesh or bones or anything holding them together but their thin delicate exoskeleton.

YOU ALWAYS TRY TO KILL ME IN YOUR DREAMS

Dreams shouldn't kill you. If you die in a dream you should be fine in real life. But that's not what Elias learns once he moves in with a girl named Roe who has the terrible habit of pulling people into her dreams with her whenever she falls asleep. Although she's the nicest, coolest, most attractive woman Elias has ever known while she's awake, Roe is a complete psychopath in her dreams. She will stop at nothing to kill anyone who finds their way into her subconscious worlds. But Elias has no choice but to survive her crazy dreams every night if he ever hopes to make it in a world that has been torn apart by a global pandemic and economic collapse.

APESHIP

An intolerable prick takes his weird daughter, his college-aged girlfriend, her douchey brother and her awkward best friend on a boating trip to show off his new yacht. But when they come across an abandoned cruise ship in the middle of the ocean, they find themselves hunted by a group of sadistic mutant killers hell-bent on keeping them as their immortal playthings for all eternity.

THE GIRL WITH THE BARBED WIRE HAIR

There is a girl who lives in the alley behind the old, abandoned fire station. She is always covered in ash and grime, cuts and bruises on her arms and legs, the skirt of her school uniform caked in dirt and ripped into tatters. Her hair is a mess of dreadlocks the color of rusted metal, growing like vines all the way down to her ankles. She was once human, but not anymore. She's become a feral creature with an undying thirst for blood and revenge. But when she meets a young boy named Yusuke, the first person to ever show her an ounce of human kindness, her desire for revenge turns to feelings of love. And she will do whatever it takes to win his heart, even if she has to rip it from his chest in order to obtain it.

SCORPION RANCH

Daniel Munch is in a toxic relationship, but not just because his girlfriend is selfish and manipulative. She is also literally toxic—born with glands in her mouth and genitals that spew deadly poison. Every time they kiss or make love, he puts his life at risk. She could kill him at any moment and he has no choice but to trust that she would never do anything to cause him harm. But when they decide to get married, Daniel is pressured into doing *the switch*—a procedure where couples swap bodies in order to better understand each other. For one month, he will become her girlfriend while she will become his boyfriend. It's only for one month, so what would be the harm in giving it a shot? Surely it wouldn't utterly destroy each and every aspect of his entire life…

EVER TIME WE MEET AT THE DAIRY QUEEN, YOUR WHOLE FUCKING FACE EXPLODES

Ethan is in love with the weird girl in school. The one with the twitchy eyes and spiders in her hair. The one who can't sit still for even a minute and speaks in an odd squeaky voice. The one they call Spiderweb.

Although she scares all the other kids in school, Ethan thinks Spiderweb is the cutest, sweetest, most perfect girl in the world. But there's a problem. Whenever they go on a date at the Dairy Queen, her whole fucking face explodes.

EXERCISE BIKE

There is something wrong with Tori Manetti's new exercise bike. It is made from flesh and bone. It eats and breathes and poops. It was once a billionaire named Darren Oscarson who underwent years of cosmetic surgery to be transformed into a human exercise bike so that he could live out his deepest sexual fantasy. Now Tori is forced to ride him, use him as a normal piece of exercise equipment, no matter how grotesque his appearance.

SPIDER BUNNY

Only Petey remembers the Fruit Fun cereal commercials of the 1980s. He remembers how warped and disturbing they were. He remembers the lumpy-shaped cartoon children sitting around a breakfast table, eating puffy pink cereal brought to them by the distortedly animated mascot, Berry Bunny. The characters were creepier than the Sesame Street Humpty Dumpty, freakier than Mr. Noseybonk from the old BBC show Jigsaw. They used to give him nightmares as a child. Nightmares where Berry Bunny would reach out of the television and grab him, pulling him into her cereal bowl to be eaten by the demented cartoon children.

When Petey brings up Fruit Fun to his friends, none of them have any idea what he's talking about. They've never heard of the cereal or seen the commercials before. And they're not the only ones. Nobody has ever heard of it. There's not even any information about Fruit Fun on google or wikipedia. At first, Petey thinks he's going crazy. He wonders if all of those commercials were real or just false memories. But then he starts seeing them again. Berry Bunny appears on his television, promoting Fruit Fun cereal in her squeaky unsettling voice. And the next thing Petey knows, he and his friends are sucked into the cereal commercial and forced to survive in a surreal world populated by cartoon characters made flesh.

SWEET STORY

Sally is an odd little girl. It's not because she dresses as if she's from the Edwardian era or spends most of her time playing with creepy talking dolls. It's because she chases rainbows as if they were butterflies. She believes that if she finds the end of the rainbow then magical things will happen to her--leprechauns will shower her with gold and fairies will grant her every wish. But when she actually does find the end of a rainbow one day, and is given the opportunity to wish for whatever she wants, Sally asks for something that she believes will bring joy to children all over the world. She wishes that it would rain candy forever. She had no idea that her innocent wish would lead to the extinction of all life on earth.

TUMOR FRUIT

Eight desperate castaways find themselves stranded on a mysterious deserted island. They are surrounded by poisonous blue plants and an ocean made of acid. Ravenous creatures lurk in the toxic jungle. The ghostly sound of crying babies can be heard on the wind.

Once they realize the rescue ships aren't coming, the eight castaways must band together in order to survive in this inhospitable environment. But survival might not be possible. The air they breathe is lethal, there is no shelter from the elements, and the only food they have to consume is the colorful squid-shaped tumors that grow from a mentally disturbed woman's body.

AS SHE STABBED ME GENTLY IN THE FACE

Oksana Maslovskiy is an award-winning artist, an internationally adored fashion model, and one of the most infamous serial killers this country has ever known. She enjoys murdering pretty young men with a nine-inch blade, cutting them open and admiring their delicate insides. It's the only way she knows how to be intimate with another human being. But one day she meets a victim who cannot be killed. His name is Gabriel—a mysterious immortal being with a deep desire to save Oksana's soul. He makes her a deal: if she promises to never kill another person again, he'll become her eternal murder victim.

What at first seems like the perfect relationship for Oksana quickly devolves into a living nightmare when she discovers that Gabriel enjoys being killed by her just a little too much. He turns out to be obsessive, possessive, and paranoid that she might be murdering other men behind his back. And because he is unkillable, it's not going to be easy for Oksana to get rid of him.

NEVERDAY

Karl Lybeck has been repeating the same day over and over again, in a constant loop, for what feels like a thousand years. He thought he was the only person trapped in this eternal hell until he meets a young woman named January who is trapped in the same loop that Karl's been stuck within for so many centuries. But it turns out that Karl and January aren't alone. In fact, the majority of the population has been repeating the same day just as they have been. And society has mutated into something completely different from the world they once knew.

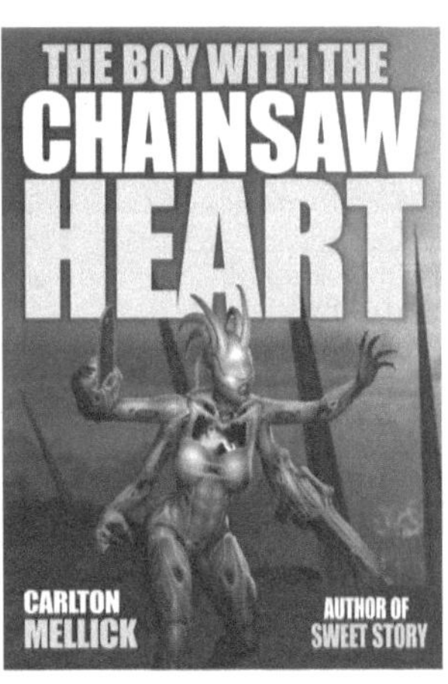

THE BOY WITH THE CHAINSAW HEART

Mark Knight awakens in the afterlife and discovers that he's been drafted into Hell's army, forced to fight against the hordes of murderous angels attacking from the North. He finds himself to be both the pilot and the fuel of a demonic war machine known as Lynx, a living demon woman with the ability to mutate into a weaponized battle suit that reflects the unique destructive force of a man's soul.

PARASITE MILK

Irving Rice has just arrived on the planet Kynaria to film an episode of the popular Travel Channel television series *Bizarre Foods with Andrew Zimmern: Intergalactic Edition*. Having never left his home state, let alone his home planet, Irving is hit with a severe case of culture shock. He's not prepared for Kynaria's mushroom cities, fungus-like citizens, or the giant insect wildlife. He's also not prepared for the consequences after he spends the night with a beautiful nymph-like alien woman who infects Irving with dangerous sexually-transmitted parasites that turn his otherworldly business trip into an agonizing fight for survival.

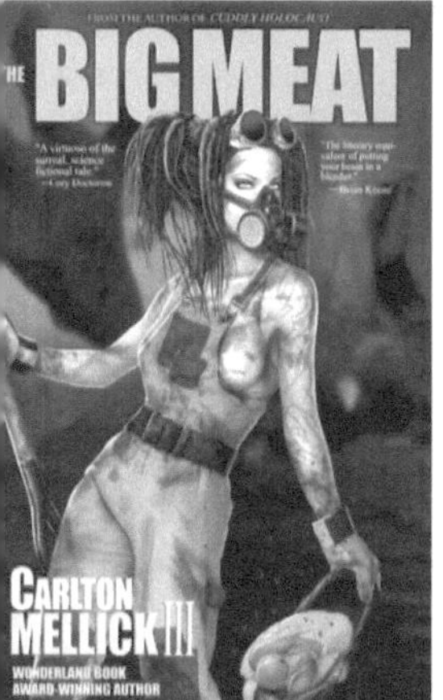

THE BIG MEAT

In the center of the city once known as Portland, Oregon, there lies a mountain of flesh. Hundreds of thousands of tons of rotting flesh. It has filled the city with disease and dead-lizard stench, contaminated the water supply with its greasy putrid fluids, clogged the air with toxic gasses so thick that you can't leave your house without the aid of a gas mask. And no one really knows quite what to do about it. A thousand-man demolition crew has been trying to clear it out one piece at a time, but after three months of work they've barely made a dent. And then there's the junkies who have started burrowing into the monster's guts, searching for a drug produced by its fire glands, setting back the excavation even longer.

It seems like the corpse will never go away. And with the quarantine still in place, we're not even allowed to leave. We're stuck in this disgusting rotten hell forever.

THE TERRIBLE THING THAT HAPPENS

There is a grocery store. The last grocery store in the world. It stands alone in the middle of a vast wasteland that was once our world. The open sign is still illuminated, brightening the black landscape. It can be seen from miles away, even through the poisonous red ash. Every night at the exact same time, the store comes alive. It becomes exactly as it was before the world ended. Its shelves are replenished with fresh food and water. Ghostly shoppers walk the aisles. The scent of freshly baked breads can be smelled from the rust-caked parking lot. For generations, a small community of survivors, hideously mutated from the toxic atmosphere, have survived by collecting goods from the store. But it is not an easy task. Decades ago, before the world was destroyed, there was a terrible thing that happened in this place. A group of armed men in brown paper masks descended on the shopping center, massacring everyone in sight. This horrible event reoccurs every night, in the exact same manner. And the only way the wastelanders can gather enough food for their survival is to traverse the killing spree, memorize the patterns, and pray they can escape the bloodbath in tact.

BIO MELT

Nobody goes into the Wire District anymore. The place is an industrial wasteland of poisonous gas clouds and lakes of toxic sludge. The machines are still running, the drone-operated factories are still spewing biochemical fumes over the city, but the place has lain abandoned for decades.

When the area becomes flooded by a mysterious black ooze, six strangers find themselves trapped in the Wire District with no chance of escape or rescue.

CUDDLY HOLOCAUST

Teddy bears, dollies, and little green soldiers—they've all had enough of you. They're sick of being treated like playthings for spoiled little brats. They have no rights, no property, no hope for a future of any kind. You've left them with no other option-in order to be free, they must exterminate the human race.

Julie is a human girl undergoing reconstructive surgery in order to become a stuffed animal. Her plan: to infiltrate enemy lines in order to save her family from the toy death camps. But when an army of plushy soldiers invade the underground bunker where she has taken refuge, Julie will be forced to move forward with her plan despite her transformation being not entirely complete.

ARMADILLO FISTS

A weird-as-hell gangster story set in a world where people drive giant mechanical dinosaurs instead of cars.

Her name is Psycho June Howard, aka Armadillo Fists, a woman who replaced both of her hands with living armadillos. She was once the most bloodthirsty fighter in the world of illegal underground boxing. But now she is on the run from a group of psychotic gangsters who believe she's responsible for the death of their boss. With the help of a stegosaurus driver named Mr. Fast Awesome—who thinks he is God's gift to women even though he doesn't have any arms or legs--June must do whatever it takes to escape her pursuers, even if she has to kill each and every one of them in the process.

VILLAGE OF THE MERMAIDS

Mermaids are protected by the government under the Endangered Species Act, which means you aren't able to kill them even in self-defense. This is especially problematic if you happen to live in the isolated fishing village of Siren Cove, where there exists a healthy population of mermaids in the surrounding waters that view you as the main source of protein in their diet.

The only thing keeping these ravenous sea women at bay is the equally-dangerous supply of human livestock known as Food People. Normally, these "feeder humans" are enough to keep the mermaid population happy and well-fed. But in Siren Cove, the mermaids are avoiding the human livestock and have returned to hunting the frightened local fishermen. It is up to Doctor Black, an eccentric representative of the Food People Corporation, to investigate the matter and hopefully find a way to correct the mermaids' new eating patterns before the remaining villagers end up as fish food. But the more he digs, the more he discovers there are far stranger and more dangerous things than mermaids hidden in this ancient village by the sea.

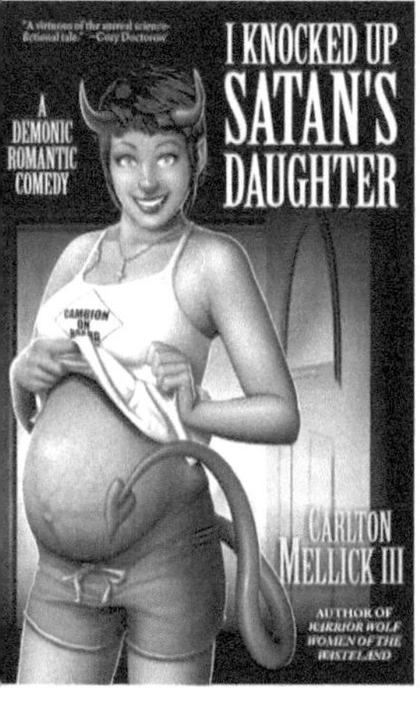

I KNOCKED UP SATAN'S DAUGHTER

Jonathan Vandervoo lives a carefree life in a house made of legos, spending his days building lego sculptures and his nights getting drunk with his only friend—an alcoholic sumo wrestler named Shoji. It's a pleasant life with no responsibility, until the day he meets Lici. She's a soul-sucking demon from hell with red skin, glowing eyes, a forked tongue, and pointy red devil horns... and she claims to be nine months pregnant with Jonathan's baby.

Now Jonathan must do the right thing and marry the succubus or else her demonic family is going to rip his heart out through his ribcage and force him to endure the worst torture hell has to offer for the rest of eternity. But can Jonathan really love a fire-breathing, frog-eating, cold-blooded demoness? Or would eternal damnation be preferable? Either way, the big day is approaching. And once Jonathan's conservative Christian family learns their son is about to marry a spawn of Satan, it's going to be all-out war between demons and humans, with Jonathan and his hell-born bride caught in the middle.

KILL BALL

n a city where everyone lives inside of plastic bubbles, there s no such thing as intimacy. A husband can no longer kiss ıis wife. A mother can no longer hug her children. To do this vould mean instant death. Ever since the disease swept across he globe, we have become isolated within our own personal ›lastic prison cells, rolling aimlessly through rubber streets in vhat are essentially man-sized hamster balls.

Colin Hinchcliff longs for the touch of another human ›eing. He can't handle the loneliness, the confinement, and ıe's horribly claustrophobic. The only thing keeping him ;oing is his unrequited love for an exotic dancer named Siren, woman who has never seen his face, doesn't even know his ıame. But when The Kill Ball, a serial slasher in a black leather phere, begins targeting women at Siren's club, Colin decides ıe has to do whatever it takes in order to protect her... even if he has to break out of his bubble and risk everything to do it.

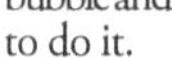

THE TICK PEOPLE

They call it Gloom Town, but that isn't its real name. It is a sad city, the saddest of cities, a place so utterly depressing that even their ales are brewed with the most sorrow-filled tears. They built it on the back of a colossal mountain-sized animal, where its woeful citizens live like human fleas within the hairy, pulsing landscape. And those tasked with keeping the city in a state of constant melancholy are the Stressmen-a team of professional sadness-makers who are perpetually striving to invent new ways of causing absolute misery.

But for the Stressman known as Fernando Mendez, creating grief hasn't been so easy as of late. His ideas aren't effective anymore. His treatments are more likely to induce happiness than sadness. And if he wants to get back in the game, he's going to have to relearn the true meaning of despair.

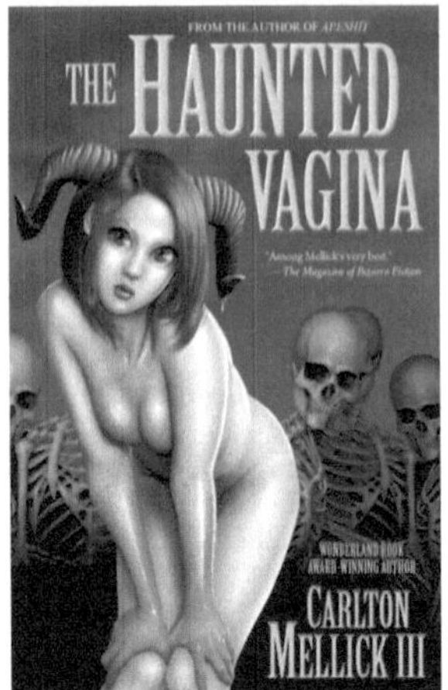

THE HAUNTED VAGINA

It's difficult to love a woman whose vagina is a gateway to the world of the dead...

Steve is madly in love with his eccentric girlfriend, Stacy. Unfortunately, their sex life has been suffering as of late, because Steve is worried about the odd noises that have been coming from Stacy's pubic region. She says that her vagina is haunted. She doesn't think it's that big of a deal. Steve, on the other hand, completely disagrees.

When a living corpse climbs out of her during an awkward night of sex, Stacy learns that her vagina is actually a doorway to another world. She persuades Steve to climb inside of her to explore this strange new place. But once inside, Steve finds it difficult to return... especially once he meets an oddly attractive woman named Fig, who lives within the lonely haunted world between Stacy's legs.

THE CANNIBALS OF CANDYLAND

There exists a race of cannibals who are made out of candy. They live in an underground world filled with lollipop forests and gumdrop goblins. During the day, while you are away at work, they come above ground and prowl our streets for food. Their prey: your children. They lure young boys and girls to them with their sweet scent and bright colorful candy coating, then rip them apart with razor sharp teeth and claws.

When he was a child, Franklin Pierce witnessed the death of his siblings at the hands of a candy woman with pink cotton candy hair. Since that day, the candy people have become his obsession. He has spent his entire life trying to prove that they exist. And after discovering the entrance to the underground world of the candy people, Franklin finds himself venturing into their sugary domain. His mission: capture one of them and bring it back, dead or alive.

THE EGG MAN

It is a survival of the fittest world where humans reproduce like insects, children are the property of corporations, and having a ten foot tall brain is a grotesque sexual fetish.

Lincoln has just been released into the world by the George Organization, a corporation that raises creative types. A Smell, he has little prospect of succeeding as a visual artist. But after he moves into the Henry Building, he meets Luci, the weird and grimy girl who lives across the hall. She is a Sight. She is also the most disgusting woman Lincoln has ever met. Little does he know, she will soon become his muse.

Now Luci's boyfriend is threatening to kill Lincoln, two rival corporations are preparing for war, and Luci is dragging him along to discover the truth about the mysterious egg man who lives next door. Only the strongest will survive in this tale of individuality, love, and mutilation.

APESHIT

Apeshit is Mellick's love letter to the great and terrible B-horror movie genre. Six trendy teenagers (three cheerleaders and three football players) go to an isolated cabin in the mountains for a weekend of drinking, partying, and crazy sex, only to find themselves in the middle of a life and death struggle against a horribly mutated psychotic freak that just won't stay dead. Mellick parodies this horror cliché and twists it into something deeper and stranger. It is the literary equivalent of a grindhouse film. It is a splatter punk's wet dream. It is perhaps one of the most fucked up books ever written.

If you are a fan of Takashi Miike, Evil Dead, early Peter Jackson, or Eurotrash horror, then you must read this book.

CLUSTERFUCK

A bunch of douchebag frat boys get trapped in a cave with subterranean cannibal mutants and try to survive not by using their wits but by following the bro code...

From master of bizarro fiction Carlton Mellick III, author of the international cult hits Satan Burger and Adolf in Wonderland, comes a violent and hilarious B movie in book form. Set in the same woods as Mellick's splatterpunk satire Apeshit, Clusterfuck follows Trent Chesterton, alpha bro, who has come up with what he thinks is a flawless plan to get laid. He invites three hot chicks and his three best bros on a weekend of extreme cave diving in a remote area known as Turtle Mountain, hoping to impress the ladies with his expert caving skills.

But things don't quite go as Trent planned. For starters, only one of the three chicks turns out to be remotely hot and she has no interest in him for some inexplicable reason. Then he ends up looking like a total dumbass when everyone learns he's never actually gone caving in his entire life. And to top it all off, he's the one to get blamed once they find themselves lost and trapped deep underground with no way to turn back and no possible chance of rescue. What's a bro to do? Sure he could win some points if he actually tried to save the ladies from the family of unkillable subterranean cannibal mutants hunting them for their flesh, but fuck that. No slam piece is worth that amount of effort. He'd much rather just use them as bait so that he can save himself.

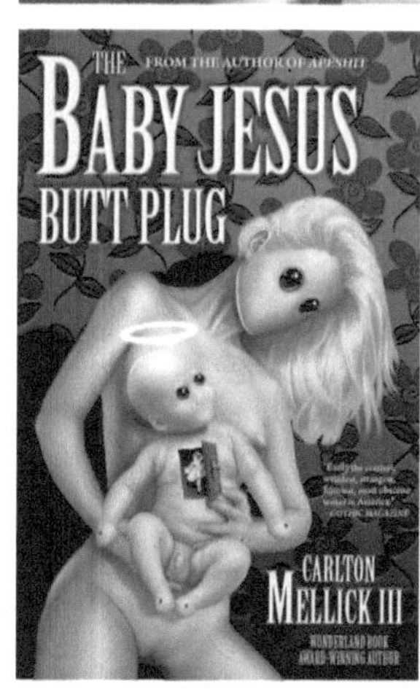

THE BABY JESUS BUTT PLUG

Step into a dark and absurd world where human beings are slaves to corporations, people are photocopied instead of born, and the baby jesus is a very popular anal probe.

www.ingramcontent.com/pod-product-compliance
Lightning Source LLC
LaVergne TN
LVHW091006080826
845145LV00003B/1151

* 9 7 8 1 6 2 1 0 5 3 6 6 8 *